ONE BROKEN
SPUR

ONE BROKEN
SPUR

NORMAN JOHN

ONE BROKEN SPUR

iUniverse books may be ordered through booksellers or by contacting:

iUniverse
1663 Liberty Drive
Bloomington, IN 47403
www.iuniverse.com
1-800-Authors (1-800-288-4677)

Because of the dynamic nature of the Internet, any web addresses or links contained in this book may have changed since publication and may no longer be valid. The views expressed in this work are solely those of the author and do not necessarily reflect the views of the publisher, and the publisher hereby disclaims any responsibility for them.

Any people depicted in stock imagery provided by Thinkstock are models, and such images are being used for illustrative purposes only. Certain stock imagery © Thinkstock.

ISBN: 978-1-5320-2557-0 (sc)
ISBN: 978-1-5320-2558-7 (e)

Library of Congress Control Number: 2017908895

Print information available on the last page.

iUniverse rev. date: 06/22/2017

This book was written with the inspiration from and dedicated to the remembrance of my friends in and out of the military, who have passed away.

My wife Thanyatorn Gornphun has given her patience, guidance, understanding and putting up with me during the writing of this book, thank you. My love for you is bigger and bigger every day. I not only love you, but I am also in love with you.

TABLE OF CONTENTS

1

"Tighten those cows up, come on Tim move it, Jeff, hustle it up, get moving much faster" Jim Flades yelled, "We have to get these two hundred or so cows out of here before the ranchers wake up. Tim, use your lasso and tear 3 or 4 good size branches off of that tree, we can drag those branches over our trail, that'll wipe all the horse and cow tracks out and throw the law dogs off our trail. That'll keep them busy for a while and give us time for a clean get away!"

Norman John is my name, and I'm the sheriff of Monark. As I look down the street in the town of Monark, nothing is moving, and all is quiet at this early hour in the crack O dark. This quiet little town of Monark is situated sixteen miles north of the town of Biggar, and 48 miles south of Battleford in North West Territories. Battleford is located on the western side of North West Territories and served as the capital of the North-West Territories until 1883. In 1883, the capital of the North-West Territories moved to Regina where it remained until 1905, this is when Regina became the capital of the newly formed province of Saskatchewan, but I am getting ahead of myself. Let me start at the beginning.

In the summer of eighteen seventy-four, I stand in the street of Monark, the day is starting out very sunny and no clouds in the sky. The streets at 5:30 in the morning are still empty, void of people, nobody in, out or about town. The only restaurant in town is owned and operated by Fred Benson, and this eatery will not open for business until 7:00 o'clock in the morning. Fred Benson will already be working in the back, lighting the stove, making coffee and Cookin a pot of pinto beans, potatoes and, getting ready to cook the steaks for this morning's breakfast. There are no horses tied to the hitching rails this early in the morning.

Nimble Fingers Selkirk or Slick Selkirk is the name we have come to know him by his moniker. He had come to us from east of here, from that rough little seedy place that would grow up and become Boom Town. Slick was friends with James Robert Wilson who is planning to a flour mill in 1902, and this man also has his sights set on politics and wants to run as overseer of Boom Town, which later became Saskatoon. Whoa, wait a minute; let me slow down and back up a bit, I'm getting ahead of myself, and, this is another story. Let's start at the beginning. Slick was a slim 6 foot even tall hombre; he was broad at the shoulder and narrow at the hip. His arms and legs had a muscular look and were the size of oversized stove pipes. His upper lip sported a bristle type mustache. The color of his face was a tanned golden brown with jet black hair and mustache. His eyes were a dark brown that changed color to a light hazel when he felt cornered, or he was about to fill his hand with a gun or an axe handle. Slick would practice with a gun every day, pulling that hunk of steel from his hip, then he would practice drawing and shooting until he felt accomplished with a gun. Slick practiced and practiced drawing, shooting, looking where he shoots and shoots where he looks. When nimble fingers felt he was good enough to his standard, he then picked up a deck of cards and practiced with the cards. Slick would add in his head as fast as he could all the card numbers, he would also practice remembering which cards were taken out of the deck and what cards were left. Slick would practice holding the cards and doing card tricks, things like pulling cards out of midair or pulling a card from behind someone's ear and sometimes even pulling a card from someone's pocket. Slick was even starting to practice dealing cards and make no mistake, he was becoming very good at cards, his fingers seemed to be a blur when he dealt the cards, and as a matter a fact, his name was even starting to be known. Later when Slick felt he had practiced enough, he asked Art Fallas, Owner of the Brigantine Saloon, "Can I use a table in the saloon to start a poker table?"

Art agreed, saying "I want a clean table, with no swindling or cheating going on; I don't want you to give the Brigantine Saloon a bad name."

Slick Selkirk ran a very clean table, and there were times men would come up and ask Slick if he would start a poker game. Slick was becoming a recognized person in the saloon, and he was also associated with words like honest, good man to have on your side, do not stand for cheats at the card table and one person was even heard to say "If Slick is in the game, then so am I." Yes, Slick was becoming popular in Monark, even the ladies would say hello to Slick when they passed each other on the boardwalk in front of various businesses, and it was the ladies that turned around to see Slick behind them. There were even a couple of times I deputized Slick to help keep the law in Monark. I remember, for example, one of those times there was this obstinate cuss who thought he should shoot up Monark. Well, you should have seen Slick, he just went over casual like, slapped that man in the face a hard wallop. Then he reached over and took his gun from him, and all this before the man could swallow, spit or turn around, the man never even knew what was going on. I was watching all this, and all I saw was Slick's hand movement, his hands were just a blur. Yes, Slick was definitely without a doubt a good addition to Monark.

Art Fallas will just be getting up now. Art had spent some time in the Canadian Navy riding in those wooden galleons, twelve years to be exact. When Art had left the Navy, he was traveling through Monark, on his way to Alaska, he liked what he saw and, at first, he stayed six months, saying "I'll only stay a little and test the water," and he has been here ever since.

Bob Little, will be in the livery stable feeding the horses, cleaning out the inside of the livery of the night housing of the Broncs. Bob had spent twenty years in the horse artillery in Upper Canada. After his military time was up, he left the horse artillery, moved to Monark, built a barn with a stable and livery attached to the side. The livery was a great addition to Monark, a horse and carriage could be rented for one dollar a day. Bob also had the only top quality, worth his salt, blacksmith with a forge in the town of Monark.

Andy John is the main man in the Blacksmith Shop. Andy stands 5' 11 inches in his sock feet, wears a size nine shoe; his hands are as big as a large dinner plate. Andy's arms are the size of your thighs. His measurements are 34 inches at the hips, 28 inches at his waist and 54 inches in his chest and shoulder area, his neck is 27 inches around, and his head is the size large, and to cover his monstrous head, he wears a ten-gallon hat. When Andy wears his two six-guns with pearl handles, the guns look very small, in his extremely large hands. When he holds the two guns, you have to look very close because it's hard to see these two guns in those large hands. Andy prefers a rifle instead of the six-guns, because his fingers are almost too big for the finger guard in the six guns. Andy John can shoot a fly off a wall at 50 feet; this man has a natural talent for shooting a rifle. When at work in the Blacksmith Shop, Andy uses a fifteen pound hammer like you and I would use a one pound hammer. One time a few years back I heard someone say they had seen Andy pick up a full grown horse with its four feet off the ground, and someone else had said they had seen Andy pick up one side of a prairie schooner and lift it clear off the ground, to replace the wheel. Andy can out-shoot, out-fight, out-work, out-ride and out-talk everybody in the area. The bottom line is, this man is big, strong and many men suggested this is a man to be respected.

Then there is me, Norman John, like I said, "I am the sheriff in Monark." I grew up in Monark, traveled to Upper Canada to join the horse artillery, and had spent five years in the horse artillery where I met Bob Little, became and stayed good friends ever since. After my five-year hitch in the Horse Artillery, I had traveled back to Monark, ran for town marshal and I won the town marshal election.

Jacqueline and Alasdair Rumsel grew up in Scotland, where Alasdair became the Town Constable. Later the Rumsel family had traveled from Scotland to Upper Canada then on towards the Alaska gold rush. The Rumsel's were traveling through Biggar, North West Territories. When they stopped for breakfast, someone had suggested they go to Monark, seems there are more jobs than people in Monark. Alasdair became Deputy Sheriff in Monark, and he has excelled at this job. Alasdair is five feet six inches tall in his bare feet. This man is big, solid and strong; he weighs three hundred and twenty pounds. Alasdair wears a size large ten-gallon hat, and his head seems to go straight to his shoulders, it looks like he has no neck. When you look at his feet, you would think it would take a whole cow to make his boots. I remember hearing somebody once say "if you weren't so turned up at the bottom, you would be a big man." Alasdair is the strongest and yet the gentlest man I've ever seen. He can lift straight up and arms straight out, three hundred pounds in each arm, yes sir, he can lift the weight straight up off the floor and over his head, and, he can also pick up a baby kitten and never hurt that little critter. Alasdair is as honest as the day is long, the only problem it seems, sometimes there is an articulation problem, and there are only a few people that can understand him, especially when he gets excited.

Jacqueline Rumsel, Alasdair's wife, she is a picture of

loveliness. Jacqueline has coal black hair, and her eyes are the deepest, biggest and most glistening pools of black orbs that I have ever seen, and these gorgeous eyes match her hair. Jacqueline is positively not hard to look at, matter a fact, just the opposite. She has an hourglass figure, and her face is so attractive that many men stand rooted where they are. They seem to be mesmerized when they look upon her very pretty face. When she speaks it sounds like angels are singing, if there is such a thing as an angel, this would fit Jacqueline. All in all, Jacqueline is one of these ladies where everything seems to be in the proper place and screams very loud to say "Hey, look at me!"

In the area a long way south of Calgras, in 1859 the local army outlawed alcohol trading, with the Indians. However, the traders John J. Healey and Alfred B. Hamilton started the whiskey trading post, Fort Hamilton near the junction of St Mary and Old Man Rivers. After the fort had burned down, they rebuilt the fort, and the nickname Fort Whoop-Up was hand picked.

The whiskey trade in Fort Whoop-up was an overly abundant substantial business, and eventually, this led to the eighteen seventy-three massacres of many Assiniboine's Indians in the Cypress Hills area by some trappers south of Calgras. As a result, the North West Mounted Police (which later became known as the RCMP, but I'm getting ahead of myself again, and that's another story) were sent to the area to stop the liquor trade, Indian killing and establish order.

My very good friend Assistant Commissioner Daryl McFidgen and I grew up together in Monark. When Daryl was 21 he left home and traveled to Biggar to join that new

Police group that began from a spark of an idea in 1873; they were traveling through Biggar in approximately late August 1874, on their way to this new little town called Calgras. Daryl always wanted excitement, and he always liked to live on the edge with his nerves tingling as he says "makes my life exciting."

The whiskey traded or sold at the Fort Whoop-up post had often been not much more than a mixture of alcohol, river water, chewing tobacco, and lye.

The Police Troop arrived at Fort Whop-Up on nine October, in eighteen seventy-four. The weary foot troop of Policemen topped a valley rim and saw what looked like a very rustic area, they were looking at two clean rivers, with forests of Spruce and Douglas Fir Trees on the shady north face, and poplars were following the river's edge. This particular parcel of land was the ideal place to build a fort, and though they could not look that far ahead or anticipate, it was also the ideal place to build a city. The policemen were foot weary because, during the trip from Upper Canada to Fort Whoop-up, most of their horses had died. The horses seemed to go loco and were so bad, and malicious tempered they were not controllable, and some of them even had to be shot.

Later in eighteen seventy-five, the Mounted Police established a post at the fort by renting a room from Healy and Hamilton. For the next twelve years, Fort Whoop-Up continued to trade and also hosted a Police Post.

When the fort was first named, the fort was first called simply "The Elbow" or "Bow River Fort," then briefly "Fort Brisebois" by Police Inspector A.E. Brisebois. This name was not acceptable to the Superior Police Officers, and

Colonel James McLeod came up with the alternate title "Fort Calgras," after his home in the Scottish Highlands. The fortuitous location of the fort used at Calgras was because of whiskey trade, and it's trading abused the Indian tribes. The town of Calgras began by forming around the fort for quite different purposes. The rich grassy foothills to the west, a vast amount of grass growing in the rolling land to the northeast, the vast amount of grassed prairie to the east and southeast. The wolf and buffalo hide is also known as the robe trade had removed the free-roaming wolf and buffalo from the grassland areas. The Canadian Government decided to use grass and cattle as a first stage in the process of colonization and opened the territory to ranching.

I remember hearing about how Calgras started out, this little town looking like most western towns, a group of wood frame houses which were one and two stories, with the occasional wooden church steeple and maybe a city hall clock tower.

The people who were about to build, they were looking for and wanted materials more fireproof than wood. The answer was found sticking out from the banks of the Bow River in several nearby locations; this was sandstone. The cool, yellow stone was not only practical but it was attractive, and for more than twenty years, the local quarries couldn't dig in the quarry fast enough to keep up with the demand. Calgras was suddenly a city with an image, "The Sandstone City" an image separate from other cities and arguably superior. Building in Sandstone became more than mere fashion, each school, bank or a private mansion built from this stone was a contribution to identity, an act of local patriotism. Then the quarries started to export the stone to places like Monark.

Bill Moonly, the banker in the town of Monark, Sandstone was used to build his bank, and the bank's location is at the north end of Main Street in Monark. Bill is always looking to entice people to put money in his bank, rather than spending it without reason. Bill's wife Faye is a sister of the two wives of the two largest cattle outfits near Monark, the McKlay Ranch, and the Slinger Ranch. Bill and Faye have two sons and a daughter. Their daughter, Marilyn is married to Dave Milner, who is not only the lawyer in town; he is also the town mayor of Monark. Bill and Faye's two son's Andy and Mark have a large ranch, with almost six thousand cows and twenty bulls on their sixty thousand five hundred and sixty-acre ranch. Both Andy and Mark were looking for an easier way to keep the cow herd on their ranch land, and had purchased a new type of wire for the ranch, "The Thorny Fence." This wire with barbs invented in Chicago by Michael Kelly in 1868. Andy and Mark had this idea, to surround their grazing fields with this thorny wire, this will help keep their cows and horses close to home without too much tribulation. The other farmers in the area had a bee in their bonnet over this idea, however. In fact, all the other farmers in the area were against the idea of putting up a fence. The Moonly ranch was next to the biggest, of the three Ranches. The Four Diamonds Moonly Ranch had acres and acres of land as far as the eye could see. You could ride in one direction all day starting at eight in the morning, and at four in the evening you would reach the other outer land marker. The Moonly Ranch held 60,560 acres and almost 6,000 Aberdeen Angus cows and one hundred head of good quality quarter horses, a superb strain of horse flesh.

The Moonly Ranch had a total of fifteen saddle pounders riding the grazing land, and they even had a new hired hand with the designation animal doctor also called the veterinarian. This type of doctor started in 1646. The veterinarian, Beth Morgan with her husband Fred lived in the Moonly's log and sandstone house, and she slept in one of the ten bedrooms. Beth stood about four foot eight inches, pretty as a picture and no bigger than a match stick. She had a hard time starting out as a veterinarian, seems the men did not accept a woman as an animal doctor. However, Beth was the best person I had ever seen anybody doctoring a horse or cow. When Beth was working, it was almost as if she could talk to the animals. To see her working was a real treat. I remember one time she had to doctor this old bull. Foam hanging out the nose holes, that old bull had sent many two hundred and fifty-pound men runnin out of that pen. Well Beth, she just climbed over the rails, walked up ever so calm like, looked like she was singing softly to that old hunk of fur. Then all of a sudden, it looked like she put one hand under the bulls head and rubbed while at the same time rubbing the side of the face under the eye. After about 1 minute, she stopped and started to walk back to us men standing and watching, well we seen the oddest thing, that old large ball of muscle, bone, and fur all wrapped up to make the most cantankerous bull you ever were seen. He just followed her just like a little puppy follering the master. That picture will always stay lodged in my think pail.

Back to the large house, the design was not only a log house construction with white chinks between the logs but also supported a sandstone construction. Andy and Mark Moonly were not only brothers and partners, but they were also best of friends. If you ever have the opportunity to walk around and take a gander, they have planned well, worked hard, and built up this large and most extravagant looking ranch that is very pleasing to the eye. The house has ten large bedrooms, a reading room, a games room for the games of chance, playing poker or other games, a parlor, a kitchen with the latest kitchen equipment and a large dining room. The staff members consisted of a butler, three maids and a cook that can make the most mouth-watering meals you ever tasted. There was even a newfangled pump in the kitchen; this is where the cold fresh water came from below ground and pumped into a bowl or pail. All you have to do is move a handle up and down quickly, then to our amazement, look! Water flows into a container! There are quarters for the staff member attached to the back side of the house. The structure alone is very and utterly impressive because Andy and Mark had started with a sod house. Hard work, planning, and vision, the ranch had been able to grow into a significant ranch with a larger more permanent house. Andy and Mark are the sons of the Banker Bill Moonly and his wife Faye, who was a sister to Bob, Jim, and Ken McKlay.

The siblings on the original McKlay Ranch were Esther, Jim, Norma, Bob, Shirley, Faye, and Ken. The

McKlay ranch, located close to six miles west of Monark, North West Territories, and twelve miles North of Biggar. Esther's Brothers have the largest ranch in the Monark area; they have 80400 acres of fertile ranch land and growing most of the chickens, eggs, vegetables, and wheat to make bread for Monark and also oats and barley for feeding livestock, as well as growing 8,450 head of Angus Doddies. The McKlay brothers even had a silver mine on their ranch. The McKlay's employed miners to dig the silver, melt the silver down and make their bullets, silverware for eating and silver decorations for the horse, saddle, and harness as well as hanging decorations from the coal oil lamp in the living room area. The silver from this mine is the purest silver that anyone has seen in a long time, and the McKlay Ranch had also started taking orders to make silverware for the rich and industrious merchants.

One of the three brothers, Jim was his name had a horse named Billy. Jim only used Billy hitched to a wagon or buggy, to go to town. The horse was so calm and well trained, Jim never had to use reins to control the horse. Jim would just say Giddyup to go, gee for left turns, haw for right turns and whoa to stop. When he was ready to come back home after the paying for the acquisitions he would say OK Billy lets go home. The horse would walk home without having to be told to go left or right, the horse it seemed, knew the way back home.

Seven in the morning brought forth many people going for breakfast at Fred's place in Monark. Bob Little, the blacksmith, walked towards Norm, Norm said "Good morning you old goat herder,"

Bob's reply was "Who are you calling old."

"You're so old, when they were thinking up the word for soil, Bob came to mind."

"What have you got going on today Bob," Norm asked.

"Bill and Faye have hired a horse and buggy to go on a picnic today if the weather stays good."

Bob and Norm sat together ready to order when the big lumbering 6 feet 6 inch Fred came up and in his very deep hoarse and coarse voice said "You two hellion brothers, whaddya want."

Both Norm and Bob said, "Brothers, we're brothers only in our hearts and minds." Then Bob and Norm asked for steak and flapjacks.

Some of the patrons had steak and eggs, even though eggs were usually saved and served on Sundays for breakfast.

Bob said, "Norm, the other day I was talking to your deputy sheriff Alasdair and his wife Jacqueline, I was asking him how he was doing in fixing up his house," I said, "Do you know how, or do you need help with the fixing of your house? When he replied, Bob said, I surely don't understand what they said. Jacqueline and Alasdair when we're together and talking, there is a definite language difference, for example, what in tarnation does "Ah dennae ken" mean, and when Alasdair and his wife started to walk away, Alasdair said "Lang may yer lum reek" what the devil does that mean. When he first said this, I thought he was making fun of me, and I almost took a swing at him; I wanted to make his eye black and blue.

Norm laughed and said "I use to be in the same fix as

you. Ah-dennae-Ken means I don't know and Lang may yer lum reek means may you live long and stay well."

"Well, I'll be jiggered; I'll finally be able to answer Alasdair when he says either of those two sayings."

Bob also asked, "Norm, when is your package arriving, and where is this coming from again?"

"Bob, I shore am getting keyed up, the package is comin here on twenty-first August, in fifteen months. In one year and three months on 21 August, the package arrives here by stagecoach. The package is comin from some place with the name Siam. The package will have taken almost one and one-half years to come here to Monark. The name of the package is Aroonsri Gornphun. I had ordered the package from the mail order catalog. You know, the catalog that began down East, you know, the book where you can order new clothes, a new stove, a new house or a new barn and on the last page, a mail order bride. As far as I can figure out this woman has four other sisters.

Bob laughed and said, "Norm, you have more nerve than a toothache, having a mail order bride, come into Monark."

Nine o'clock, breakfast finished, most of the people were going to their place of business, and this also brought Norm's brother Lance John out, and, he'll be heading towards his mercantile shop. Lance's mercantile shop had grown from a small shop to a large mercantile store area and sold everything from ladies and men's clothing, hats and boots, horseshoes to Rooster and Zig Zag Cigarette Papers with Bull Durum and Vogue tobacco, rock candy for the kids as well as prairie schooners and farm plows.

Lance said, "If I don't have it, I will special order in just for you, each and every one of you is an important customer, I will grow by one customer at a time."

He even special ordered in a piano a few years back, the piano was for Art Fallas in the saloon. Lance even has enough bright red paint in his store to paint every building in Monark three times over.

Dave Milner was the big wig, high mucky muck in Monark, he was the Town Mayor of Monark, and he also had a business in town; his appellation said "Best Lawyer This Side Of Boom Town. Many people were heard to say, "Dave has the sharpest and fastest mind a person could ever expect to see or want in a lawyer."

I have seen for myself, If you were on the wrong side of Dave, you could end up owing more than you could pay and he would take your ranch or house in payment. More than one person felt he had been fleeced, but the bottom line is "He Is Very Good At His Trade."

Stuart Warres owned the lumber yard located in the most southern part of the town. Stuart sold everything from nails to rough 2x4's, 2x8's and rough 1x6 inch boards, Shiplap, tongue, and groove, all wood was 16 feet long and don't forget Portland cement, invented in 1824. Stuart had married Norma John. Norma was the mother of Norman and Lance John. Norma's first husband was killed by a group of bank robbers when her son Norman John had just turned 12 years old on September 15. From that moment on Norman had always said he wanted to be a law dog.

2

Most of the buildings in the town of Monark, built of wood except for the mayor's house, this fine house crafted of cement and stones for the main or first floor and wood on the roof. Even the sheriff's office and jail were built of wood, with steel bars inside the window frame to keep prisoners in, and also, keep the unwanted out.

The Monark School, located at the northern end of town, on the southwest side of the crossroads of north/south and east/west roads. The school had two teachers and taught grade 1 to 10 and was also used for a town meeting room and a dance hall whenever the special occasion came about for a shindig.

At a shindig, which usually started about six in the evening, Bill Moonly would get out his fiddle, he would stomp with his left foot 3 times, and then he would start a see-en and a saw-en on his fiddle. Lance John would bring out his squeeze box. Art Fallas would bring over his piano. Dave Milner would start calling out the dance moves. Everyone would get up and dance, even the youngsters as young as ten, would get up and shake a leg. There would be a whoop-en, a holler-en, and a stomp-en, the people, had the best of time anybody could imagine. When the clock struck nine at night, everybody stopped dancing, and lunch was set up. Some people would bring cold chicken already cooked, some would bring potatoes, somebody else would bring cooked beef ribs or stew, somebody else would bring bread and lettuce, and fresh coffee brewed. After consuming the meal, dancing was set in motion again. Between twelve o'clock and two in the morning, everyone who was dancing and stomp-en by this time felt they were starting to tire, and all were ready to go Home. Bill Moonly was tired of playing his fiddle, and Dave Milner's voice was starting to become hoarse from calling the dances for so long. Lance and art were tired of playing the squeeze box and piano, and everyone slowly rambled home from the night fun and frivolity.

The McKlay Ranch was oldest and largest of all. The matriarch, use to walk to Naseby, pick up a fifty-pound bag of flour then walk back home. The McKlay house was the biggest and most lavish in the area. The house started like many others on the prairies, it started as a sod house and later upgraded to a larger wooden structure. When they upgraded and built the McKlay permanent house, the structure was built in a large square with a thirty-foot by a thirty-foot courtyard in the center. Right smack dab right in the center, constructed with Portland cement; there was a 10-foot long by 10-foot wide, the 10-foot deep, large fish pond in the courtyard was a sight to see for sure! All rooms in the house were accessible from the courtyard. When you entered the front sixty foot by thirty-foot structure, this was the kitchen, dining room, games room, and their den. The left sixty foot by thirty-foot structure was Jim and Nedie's bedroom, parlor and sewing room with built in closets. The right sixty foot by thirty-foot structure was Bob and Joan's bedroom, parlor and Joan's sewing room and built in closets. The rear sixty foot by thirty-foot structure was Ken's living quarters, reading room and den where he kept track of all the chicken and garden tallies he looked after. All bedrooms had a walk in closet with built in shelves and coat hooks for their clothes, hat trees for their cowboy hats, shelves specially made for their boots, and built in dressers for their finest shirts, pants, and scarfs. Everything in the walk in closet, hand built with cedar wood. Strategically placed, there was also a wood and coal burning fireplace, these were built in each of the four wings to have heat in the winter time.

The house built for the McKlay's parents crafted with pride, built out of cedar logs. This log house was a gift from all the McKlay siblings to their parents and was situated and attached to the right side on the front of the enormous house; this large manor, located on a circular driveway. When you drove up to the house area, first you would come to the parent's house. To the left of the parent's house was the sibling Jim, Bob and Ken's house door entrance. Each of the house areas and the wings in the main house had a well in the house, this new fangled pump system to bring water into each house.

Jim, Bob, and Ken have the farm and ranch area that sold vegetables, chickens, and beef.

Jim was five foot eleven, clean shaven with a large toothy grin. When he smiled, you instantly felt a closeness to this man, because of this, he was able to make more contracts or buy and sell more livestock, especially with strangers than the other two brothers.

Bob was five foot eight, and he had a heavy whisker growth and even had hair growing on his finger knuckles. Bob was able to think faster in numbers than the other two brothers, and he could also cipher a column of numbers faster than a person could write down the numbers, faster than the other two brothers could cipher.

Ken was six feet even, very slim with eyes that seemed to bore right through you when he looked at you and what he hated most was to see a large person pick on a smaller one; he would stand up for those that could not stand up for themselves, this came from his Sheriffing days. Ken had been a sheriff south of Calgras, working for Judge Roy Bean, in fact, if you were to ask the judge, he would say very loudly, "Ken was next to the best sheriff I ever had." Ken was broad at the shoulder and narrow at the hip and strong as an ox. All three brothers were stronger than the average man. The men would even have competitions between themselves to determine who could lift the most.

All three men wore the same size cowboy boot, size nine to be exact.

Both Jim and Bob were married, Ken was not married, not even a girlfriend. On the ranch, Ken's job was the biggest of all, and He had a staff of 10 plus himself to tackle the large daily chores. Ken and his staff looked after and administered to five thousand chickens in the chicken barn. All the chores included egg production and gathering, chicken hatching and culling as well as the garden area. Ken's total day consisted of making sure the chicken barn was secure and no holes in the walls or floors. Had to keep the chicken eating varmints out, and making sure the yearly 5000 chicken quota maintained at all times. The chickens in the hatching area looked after very diligently, new stock of chickens were grown to replace the older or missing chickens with new stock. There is also the daily collecting eggs from the chicken laying barn area, and stripping the old laying hens from the chicken barn to sell to Fred Benson for his restaurant in Monark. Ken and his staff also looked after the feeding of all the chickens in all the chicken barn areas and looking after the farm vegetable garden area for growing everything from potatoes to carrots. Ken was always trying to improve in the barn and even have it so the chicken barn would run by itself for seven days. He even went so far as to fabricate a self-feeder system for the chickens that would feed the chickens for a week without intervention.

Jim and Bob every once in a while, would take a chicken from the barn without Ken knowing it. The brothers would pluck and clean this bird. They would put the chicken on top of the house chimney to smoke and slowly cook this bird. The daily count of Ken's chickens would not tally, and Ken was always looking for that misplaced chicken that got away and investigated how the chicken got away. Ken's conniving brothers were around the corner eating the chicken, and a tee hee-en at the prank they pulled on their little brother.

Jim and Bob were the main kingpins on the McKlay Ranch and kept all the rest of the hired hands working and looking after the Approximately 8,450 Angus Doddies, and keeping a tally of how many cows, steers, heifers, and bulls were in the lush grass farmland. Bob looked after the four corrals, one used for specialized cow breeding, one used for newly purchased heifer breeding, one used for cross breeding of the different cow breeds, and the last used for breaking horses.

Jim's job is responsible for the types of bull breeds, and the number of Black Angus bulls. The time of the year for branding. Jim also kept a tally of how many bulls, cows, heifers, steers, and calves were in each of the twenty fields and when to rotate animals from one field to the other.

One warm summer day, Jim, Bob, and Ken had gone to Monark Mercantile for a few odds and ends needed in the house. On the way back home Jim stopped the horse and buggy, Jim and Bob had gotten off to pick flowers for their wives, leaving Ken in the buggy to hold the horse. When Jim and Bob had picked enough flowers, they started towards the horse and buggy, just before they got close enough to the horse and buggy to climb on up, Ken started the horse and buggy going faster. When Jim and Bob started running Ken made the horse run. Ken made Jim and Bob walk the 4 miles home. When all three had arrived into the ranch yard, both Jim and Bob taught Ken a lesson about his doing right and wrong with the horse and buggy. There were arms and legs flying every which way, both Jim and Bob were yelling instructions while their fists were making contact, Ken was yelling to stop, and he yelled promises of "He wouldn't do that again." When all three finally stopped, Jim and Bob were chuckling amongst themselves, and Ken had bruises from his shoulders to his waist front and back. Even though this had taken place, and, if it came right down to it, all three brothers were as thick as hair on a dog's back. Nobody came in between these three brothers. Matter a fact all 3 were not only brothers, but they were also best friends. Jim, Bob, and Ken even dressed the same, they wore black pants, black double breasted button shirt with a red scarf tied around their neck hung on the left side with the scarf ends touching the left shoulder. A well formed black cowboy Stetson and a shining black gun belt with a Colt 45 hung in the holster. Shiny Silver Coloured Bullets filled all cartridge loops. When these three walked into town, they were a spectacle to behold, and most people stopped to watch them swagger down the street. Even the young twelve and thirteen-year-old boys tried to dress up and look like the McKlay brothers. The young men in Monark saw these brothers as an important somebody, and almost all the teenagers wanted to be like them in one way or another. The brothers could articulate well, they stood tall with backs straight, wide at the shoulder and narrow at the hip, and they were the pinnacle of politeness.

3

The Slinger Ranch, Faye's sister, Esther is married to Hubert Slinger, and the ranch area is 406,000 acres of lush grassland for their 46,000 head of Hereford cattle. On the Slinger spread, the hired hand count was 25 cowhands in peak time, to ride the range and look after all their Herford cows in the herd, and spring time is the busiest with rounding up all the herds, separating young from old and branding all the new additions to the heard.

Hubert Slinger started the Oak Leaf Ranch, and rumor had it that Hubert had befriended John Chism, William Bonnie, The Earp Brothers and Pat Garret, and, he had even sat down and smoked a peace pipe with Geronimo and Chief Navarone Stand With A Fist. Hubert had married Esther McKlay sister to Fay, Norma, Shirley and Bob, Jim and Ken McKlay. Hubert's wife Esther, her two sons, were the most precious to her, and both Hubert and Esther were profoundly proud of them. Her children caused Esther to walk with a purpose, and her head held just a mite taller when she thought of the two boys. The two boys were married, and both boys were wide at the shoulder and narrow at the hip. Murray was married to

Ricki and Maurice was married to Lorie. The two brothers complimented each other on the ranch. Murray could ride anything that had four legs. In fact, it was as if Murray had glue on his britches when he jumped in the saddle; nothing could take Murray out of the saddle unless he decided the ride is finished. Maurice had that uncanny natural knack of being able to hold his hand out and everything that flew, walked, slithered or crawled would come up to Maurice. He would hold his hand out to a new unbroken horse that came to the ranch, the horse would walk up and eat grain from Maurice's hand, he would then put a halter over the horse's head and the horse never even flinched. The two boys designed and built a saddle from many layers of heavy canvas and a bridle with reins made from a rope that could be used in water and unlike leather, this would never shrink because of being wet with water. They would take the horse to a deep water hole, Maurice would saddle the horse in the water, and Murray would jump in the saddle and away the two would go as Jim McKlay once said, "look at them two, horse and rider put's on a very good show." The horse would splash around, jumping up and down, side to side, this way and that. When the day's work of breaking the horse to ride in the water, they found that doing it this way, Spurs never touched the horse. Using this technic still left the horse with ambition and never impeded the horse's think bucket.

Hubert was six foot tall, full head of hair, clean shaven, eyes the color oak tree trunks, and had more nerve and energy than ten men put together. He could lift a one-year-old bull off the ground, throw an ax forty feet and hit a bull's eye, and with his Winchester, he could out shoot most men. Hubert insisted he only worked from first daylight to sundown, dark was his time to be home with his family. Sunday was Hubert's time to hitch the horse to the buggy; he would take his wife, both sons and their wives out on a day's outing to look at other Farms, Ranches, and various areas, as well as towns, he had never been to before. At harvesting time when Hubert was doing his ranching duties, Hubert would work about sixteen hours a day weather permitting. Once a year Hubert and Esther would have a family gathering and roast a young calf for all his neighbors and family members to eat and have a pure and simple frivolity day.

In the area of the Oak Leaf Ranch, yard site, there were also five corrals. The first corral was for the string of new horses to be broken to ride. The second corral was for Hubert's passion of breeding a new strain of horse flesh. The third corral was for the local community and the army to come in and look. They could buy some of the best horseflesh this side of Boomtown, and now, just maybe he would be able to sell horses to this new group the Mounted Police officers. The police would need to replace the horses that had died on the trail from Upper Canada heading to the new little town of Calgras. The fourth corral was for new cows and bulls, these bovines comin to the ranch needed to be in quarantine before being placed together with the other animals. Last but not least the fifth corral was for sick animals to be sent to and relegated away from the rest of the herd. Placing the sick animal in the corral would let everyone monitor the sickest stock, as well as keeping the sick away from the healthy stock. Hubert Slinger had 406,000 acres of lush broom grass for his 46,000 head of Hereford cattle, not included were fifty Purebred Hereford bulls. Hubert's fields were broken up into twelve, hundred acre fields with one thousand animals to roam each of these field areas. Hubert also had 35 cowhands in peak spring period, one hundred and fifty horses and an old, grizzly cook by the name of George Crossley, also known by the name of "cookie." Some have said this old grizzly cook, named George, could roast tree leaves and make them taste good. George could cook a beef steak so that it was very tender, so tender in fact; you could cut the steak with a fork. It seems this old cook had finished his hitch in the army when they were chasing down Geronimo and William Bonnie (Billie The Kid). After his hitch, he had heard about the Alaska Gold Rush and thought he would give the gold rush a try. On his way to Alaska, he was passing through Biggar. He liked Biggar and the area so much he stayed on for a while and was hooked ever since.

Hubert and Esther both worked hard to make what they had. Sometimes they did without to be able to save, plan, then go to town and pay with cash for what they wanted, and not borrow from the bank. They planned and tried hard to pay with cash for everything they planned for on their ranch. Hubert and Esther, like a lot of ranchers, believed that to have and keep what they have, they must work hard and plan well or they will lose it. In the early years, Hubert had even taken on other jobs to bring in money. Hubert and Esther decided to do this so they could pay with cash and not run up credit anywhere. One of the jobs he had taken on was being a buffalo hunter, he shot the buffalo for the robe, and then he took the carcasses to Chief Navarone Stand With A Fist for the all the chief's people to use and eat. On one occasion when Hubert was out hunting, the buffalo started to stampede; Hubert saw the stampede was going straight towards Chief Navarone Stand With A Fist and Ramon Thunder Cloud the chief's medicine man, in the hunting party. Chief Navarone Stand With A Fist had sprained his left leg and couldn't walk, and he was laying on a travois. Hubert was able to turn the stampede of buffalo that was comin straight towards the Indian hunting party; Then he led the horse and travois off to the side. There were some buffalo that ran past the Indian Chief and Stands With A Fist. From that point on, Chief Navarone Stand With A Fist always protected Hubert whenever Hubert was on Indian land. Whenever Hubert came to Chief Navarone Stand With A Fist's lodge, a peace pipe was brought out, Kinni Kenneck was stuffed into the pipe bowl by Ramon Thunder Cloud the medicine man, then Jammed, slammed, and pounded his feet up and down. He sang and wailed holding the peace pipe, then up from chest level to above his head rose the peace pipe, and he offered to the four directions North, South, East, and West. Then he lit the pipe and gave it to Chief Navarone Stand With A Fist who then drew in three puffs of smoke and passed around the peace pipe to Hubert first, who also drew in 3 puffs of smoke from the pipe to solidify peace and friendship. Hubert then passed the piece pipe to Ramon Thunder cloud who Smoked the peace pipe in the same fashion and then passed the piece pipe to other lower station Indians. Kinni-Kinnick was the small film between the bark and the wood of red willow bush, the film was scraped off and dried, ensuring not to scrape the wood, the wood made the smoke taste bad.

There was another time as Hubert tells it, when He was way down south, south of Calgras, as he had said, "It was hotter than the hubs of Lucifer's house." He had walked into the saloon for a whiskey and had noticed there was a table of four, playing cards. As Hubert tells it, He walked to the bar, ordered his whiskey and stood there sipping the cooler than lukewarm drink and just taking in the sights. All of a sudden this no-good, low-down polecat came a wobbling and weave-in into the bar, he was a swayin to and fro, and a wavin his colt 45, threatening this man he called Pat Garret. The man was saying how Pat Garret and Billy The Kid were in cahoots, cheating at cards the way they were, and he was going to shoot Pat and Billy, and then he would drag their dead bodies through town behind a horse until the clothes are torn off their backs. Hubert walked up behind the man who seemed to be drunker than a skunk. Hubert, he just picked up his 45 and clunk. He laid that gun on the side of the drunk man's head behind his ear, the drunk man's legs seemed to fold up and down he went like a sack of potatoes. Well, sir, from that point on Pat Garret and William Bonnie thought Hubert to be a pretty good fellow to be around. Wild Bill Hickok was the town sheriff; he came into the saloon and saw the fellow lying on the floor, Pat and William explained to Wild Bill what had happened. To this day, every once in a while even yet, Wild Bill would send Hubert a telegraph just to say hello.

As Hubert tells it, "These are the things I live by. I'm just being me, no more no less. Don't try to take what's not yours. Work hard, let the gears in that think bucket on your shoulders work to think with, not just lay there to hold your shoulders together. Also important is treat people with respect."

Where ever Hubert went, people would gather around him, just to listen to what he has to say. On one of those occasions somebody told a joke, well Hubert listened, when the joke was told, and people were a laughing, Hubert he sounded his laugh with a hooo-hooo-hooo, and then would ask "How do you remember all that, how do you remember all those jokes?"

On the way back from one of his buffalo hunting trips he stopped in one place south of Calgras. Well, he has seen a horse there, to Hubert this was the best lookin horseflesh he had seen in a long while. The horse's coat shone like a mirror; the legs were long, the eyes were not too close together, the muscle definition was superbly placed and could the horse run. Well, he bought that horse and brought it back to his Oak Leaf Ranch. Hubert put that mare in with his best stud. He started a new string of horse flesh, a horse that was good to look at, a horse that can think, a horse that can run faster than the wind can blow, a horse that can be taught to round up or cut out cows. A horse that can stand still with a rope thrown over the cow's head, and a horse that with its sights pointed toward a cow, the horse would stay close and cut the cow out of the herd. Most important, a horse that can pull a cow out of mud, and still have lots of spunk left.

Yes, sir, Mister Hubert Slinger had himself one extra sleek, good looking piece of horseflesh, with more horse sense than some people had sense. People would come out to his ranch just to see this new type of horse, whether it was eating or working.

When asked if he would sell the horse, his only answer was "First comes my wife and me, then we'll think of you. First, I have to look after my family and our ranch. We need this steed to chase after our herd of cows."

One day Hubert had said to Esther "The house is good, but I need another room built on, this one is to make an office. I would like to buy wood, nails, and Portland cement from Stuart Warres's Lumber Yard and paint from the Monark Mercantile; I can also invite the neighbors to help me build this. We can have us an old style barn raising party."

"Good idea, we have the money in the bank, we can buy extra tools to build this, do you know what tools and what material you'll need, you speak, and I'll write the list out for you."

"Tools needed are one square, four hammers, three square mouth spades, two hoes, three pails, two water trough's, these tools will be used to build the room."

"What about the materials, what materials do you need?"

"One hundred 2x4's, fifty 2x8's, one hundred and fifty tongue and groove boards, two panes of glass and one door, for the inside of the house, 40 bags of Portland cement, 3 pounds of nails and 3 gallons of red paint."

Esther said, "I need some odds and ends from Monark, can we go into Monark tomorrow, take the money from the bank and pay for everything you need for this extra room."

"Good idea, I'll ask the neighbors if they can help

build this starting day after tomorrow." Then Hubert asked "Esther, can you make dinner for everybody that'll be here to help build this room?"

"I'll pick up a couple of extra things in Monark, and then I'll have enough to make a meal for a large group with all the fixings, how does roast beef, gravy, potatoes and turnip sound."

"Good idea, your roast beef is the talk of the community."

When they arrived in Monark, a day in town was more than just shopping; it was also a place to meet and discuss with other ranchers or farmers, to find out how the herds are doing, the grass and how it's growing, the water level, the price of cows and more. Most of the ranchers and farmers were all very interested in how the other guy is doing. The meeting and discussing seemed to be a gauge marker on how the country was doing and what each ranch or farmer would have to do to be able to keep his head above water so to speak.

Hubert went to the mercantile and ordered paint, Lance told how much this would cost, and he told Lance "I'll be right back to pay for this." Then he went to the lumber yard and gave the list to Stuart. Stuart added up what the cost would be and gave it to Hubert. Hubert then said "Thanks, I'll be right back to pay for this," and then Hubert walked to the bank to take the money out to pay for all the tools, equipment and materials, and so off he went again to the stores to pay for and pick up everything he wanted.

Lance said "Hubert, do you need help to build the extra room? I think I can find some people here to come out to your ranch and work for you to help build your extra room."

"No thanks Lance, I am having an old fashioned barn raising bee, my neighbors have agreed to come and help me, then later I will go help them with their projects."

When the neighbors did come to help out, they had the room built in 1 and 1/2 days, and they raved about how good Esther's cooking was and wondered out loud why Hubert wasn't double his size.

4

On the start of this day, the morning was warm; the sky was the nicest blue a color you have ever seen, not a cloud in the sky. Jim Slowkem and Ray Messier were riding pastures today at the McKlay Ranch pastures. Jim was looking for sick animals, and both Jim and Ray were taking the cow tally. Jim and Ray had the Tally from last week riding in this pasture area and were comparing last week to this week tally. When the men had completely ridden all the pasture areas, the livestock count did not match; there was a notable difference in the tally numbers from last time to this time. At first, Ray thought they might have made a mistake counting the herd. There were 58 cows short in the tally. 58 cows at 10 dollars a head tally out to $580.00, a sum nothing to sneeze at, this is a good sum of money. Cattle rustling, this is the second time in six months that the cow tally comes up short. Both Jim and Ray agreed that just maybe, the idea Hubert Slinger had, about forming a Cattlemen Association was not a bad idea. Cattle and Horse rustlers, we still hang them in this area, even though the town sheriff's and the Police are trying to stop the vigilante hanging.

Jim said, "We will have to brief both Jim and Bob McKlay of this cow number shortage.

Ray said, "maybe we can put the idea into Jim and Bob's head that the Monark Deputy Sheriff would be a good one to track down the rustlers."

Jim thought that was the best idea Ray has had in weeks, and just maybe Alasdair will be worth his salt tracking those owl hoots.

Before Jim and Ray started to ride back to the McKlay ranch, they thought it would be a good idea to see where the cows run off the McKlay ranch land. When they arrived at the farthest east and most southern point of the property, close to Curts Hill School Road, both Jim and Ray lost the tracks.

Ray dismounted from his horse and scouted the area on foot, as Ray walked his jingle bobs on his Spurs made a tinkling sound. No matter how much they looked, they could not find where the tracks went from McKlay Land. Jim suggested "looks like somebody used a tree branch to brush over the cattle prints. This shore looks like a well-planned job of cattle rustling."

After riding all the pasture areas, Jim and Ray headed for the McKlay Ranch Headquarters to give the unpleasant news to Jim and Bob McKlay.

Ray said "I shore think we'd be a might better off to suggest this new deputy sheriff track down the stolen herd. From what I hear, this new deputy sheriff is betterin an Injun for tracking and followin, and what do you think we send word to one of them Regulators from way down south of here, maybe one of them can come help the boss out?"

"Now you're talkin," Ray chirped and added, "what a good idea, A Regulator! Use a regulator to find the cattle rustlers, end of the problem, never see the rustler again."

Both Ray and Jim agreed that both the bosses, Jim, and Bob might like the idea of the Deputy Sheriff and a Regulator, these men can find the Rustlers.

As Ray and Jim rode into the ranch headquarters yard, they saw both Jim and Bob McKlay walking towards the corrals. Ray called to both Jim and Bob and explained the cow tally and the number loss.

Bob McKlay suggested Ken should be invited to join them, and the five of them can go to the kitchen, there we can sit around the kitchen table, have a cup of coffee and discuss this matter. Bob sent word to Ken at the chicken house asking Ken to join them for a meeting in the kitchen.

As they all sat down at the kitchen table, Jim McKlay ran the meeting, and Jim said "Ray, can you expound on what has transpired on your ride checking the cow tally."

"Bob, Jim and Ken McKlay, this is what we had seen this morning riding all the pasture areas, counting all the cows to make a tally when we added all numbers up, there was a shortage of 58 cows from the last tally to this. At first, Jim Slowkem and I thought we made an error in counting the livestock. Jim and I checked our numbers again, all the numbers in Jim's book and my book were the same, this told us the cows were missing, and I suspect taken by some no good cattle rustlers. My way of thinking Alisdair Rumsel, the deputy sheriff in Monark, he is the best person to track these cattle rustlers. Also, a telegraph can be sent to the Marshal way south of here, ask if a Regulator could be located and would he be willing to come up to Monark, in North West Territories and track these cattle rustlers. The regulator would do this for a fee of course, and the regulator could contact Bob or Jim McKlay at the Monark telegraph office."

Everyone agreed the regulator was one option that could be drawn upon later if needed.

Both Jim and Bob Rode over to the Slinger Ranch, 5 miles away to the west, to ask Hubert Slinger if they had lost any cows due to Rustlers.

Hubert replied with a definite and loud "Yes! I have lost approx 62 cows due to rustlers."

Bob explained to Hubert the number of cows they had lost and that they were going into Monark to ask the deputy sheriff if he could help and track the rustlers. Hubert went on further to explain; he thought sending word to Austin, Texas requesting help from a regulator is a last resort.

Bob Said, "Gentlemen, this is the last resort with cows missing again, The three of us, Jim, Ken, and myself, the McKlay Ranch owners in the county of Monark would send a telegram looking for a regulator to track these rustlers down and bring them to justice dead or alive."

Hubert asked Bob if he could get in on this deputy sheriff and regulator business and that he would put in half the money required to pay for these two professional men.

Both Jim and Bob thought this was a great idea, somebody else to help pay the bills, and also, we can have another opinion to ponder on.

Bob asked Jim and Hubert "What about asking Calamity Jane if she would consider taking on the job of finding the rustlers, she's a good shooter ."

Hubert added, "Not a good idea, Calamity Jane is known for being a frontier woman, a scout and has even fought Indians, I'm thinking, to chase cattle rustlers, she will not be as good as others would be."

Jim suggested, "What about Wild Bill Hickok; he has been a scout, a soldier, a lawman, and a gunfighter, just maybe Wild Bill will come to Canada, for a fee of course."

Bob added, "In early 1871 Wild Bill was on the move, I think he was chasing down John Wesley Harden, maybe he will come to Monark."

Hubert recommended that a telegraph is sent lookin for wild Bill and see if he will come out here and work with our Deputy Marshal here in Monark.

Both Jim and Bob thought that was a plum doozy of an idea and said thanks to Hubert for his good ideas and we should all get in contact with the mayor in Monark and have a town meeting. Jim and Bob mounted their horses and started their trip to Monark.

Bob suggested they ride through Oban to Monark, Oban is just a bulge in the road, and this would take away a few miles, and this trail was also well known and used on a daily basis, and off they went, at a slow trot to save the horses.

Jim quizzed Bob asking if he knew of any cattle rustlers in Biggar, Monark, and surrounding areas.

Bob had suggested they send a few telegraphs out to many towns including Boom Town, looking for information as well as possible names of cattle rustlers.

When they arrived in Monark, both Jim and Bob McKlay met up with me. I'm the Sheriff of Monark.

Bob said "sheriff you old leather necked tyrant, how are you."

I'm good, if I were any better you old owl hoot, you and I would be brothers, and you my fine feathered friend how are you?

Bob passed on about the cattle rustling on the McKlay and the Slinger Ranches.

"I have more to add to that list. The small farmers that have less than 100 cows are also having cattle rustling going on in their spreads."

Jim added "The McKlay Ranch, the Slinger Ranch, and others are getting together for a town hall meeting. A meeting to discuss if a regulator south of Calgras, can be enticed and come down to try to find out who is taking all the cattle. We might even go so far as to ask Wild Bill Hickok; maybe he would come to Monark Canada to help us out up here and possibly even set up a cattlemen's association."

"I have an idea, why don't you include all the small farmers and ranchers in your plan as well, by including everyone, then the rustlers would be going against a large organization."

Bob thought this was a good idea and said: "Can we get the word to everyone that we're having a meeting in the school house, starting three days from now, and be seated by seven at night."

Jim added, "Can we use your Deputy Sheriff; I hear he is the best tracker we have in this area."

"You shore can use Alasdair when I see him I will pass on to him that there is a meeting at the school house in three days starting seven at night."

Bob said, "Thanks for your help Norm, was good to see you again, by the way, when is that package coming again?"

I said to both Jim and Bob "Aroonsri Gornphun comes into Monark, on the stage, the 21st of August next year, about a year and a half yet, and, you know I am starting to get excited. I saw her picture and let me tell you; she is some looker, I'll have a full-time job keeping you roosters away from her."

All three laughed with Norm because all three knew both Jim and Bob were the happiest married there ever was.

As Jim and Bob were leaving to go back to the McKlay Ranch, they shook hands with Norm and said their good-byes.

When Jim and Bob arrived back at the McKlay Ranch, they passed on to Ken McKlay what had transpired. Ken agreed with both Jim and Bob, and also added that he would like to attend the meeting taking place at the Slinger Ranch and the school house in three days in Monark with Sheriff Norman John.

Ken also passed on to Jim and Bob how the chicken barn and the garden were coming along, especially the chicken flock staying at five thousand birds, with egg production up.

Both Jim and Bob were impressed and surprised and said "well done little brother, you are doing the job of three people and doing it well, mom and dad will be very proud of you. As you know, every Sunday dinner, we discuss the goings on and pass all the information on to mom and dad, this time, mom and dad will hear how good you are doing."

Ken was starting to realize his tireless efforts and plans are beginning to pay off, using a rigid guide to working.

The money Ken makes, selling chickens, eggs, and vegetables, he can keep some which give him jingle in his pockets, and he always has a jingle in his pockets lately.

When the three days came around, Bob, Jim, their wives, and Ken traveled into Monark, to attend the meeting at the school house. All the small farmers and ranchers, as well as the McKlay, Slinger, and Moonly Ranchers were in attendance at this meeting.

When everyone had taken a seat, Dave Milner banged his wooden hammer and said, "Let this meeting come to order. To start off, Jim McKlay needs to bring everybody up to date. The chair recognizes Jim McKlay."

Jim walked to the front where Dave Milner was standing. Jim smiled his best, biggest, and whitest, shining toothy smile. Jim said in his most officious voice, "Let me bring everybody up to date, we have had some more cattle rustled again. All of us here in this room have had some or all of our cows rustled. We had horses stolen; we had our property burnt or broken into, and personal items stolen. I propose that all of us here in this room join in a Cattlemen Association, the purpose of this would be to have a large force to chase after the rustlers as well as having eyes everywhere." Jim also added "I suggest that a regulator and Wild Bill Hickok be contacted to see if they will come to help, catch or stop all cattle rustlers" then Jim sat down.

Dave Milner banged his hammer and said: "The Chair recognizes the Sheriff of Monark, Norman John."

I walked up to where Dave is standing and said "Everybody here knows my Deputy Marshall Alisdair Rumsel, and you also know he is the best tracker this side of Boom Town, Alasdair is available to help everyone at this meeting by tracking the rustlers where ever they go. Jim and Bob McKlay and I have been talking; we'll send a telegraph and ask for a regulator or Wild Bill Hickok if one of them or maybe both would consider comin this far to track rustlers and bring them to justice, anybody have any questions?"

Mark Moonly stood up and said, "Anybody with more brains than a Gophers brain bucket knows this will take longer than two weeks for Wild Bill to go from where he is. Monark is a nice town, are you sure you want to attract this kind of man into our community, I heard he was a gunfighter?"

I said "As a matter a fact Wild Bill was a gunfighter, he was also a sheriff, a soldier, and a scout,

Wild Bill has three traits that we can use. A scout to read tracks, a gunfighter to stop the rustlers and a sheriff to bring the rustlers to justice."

Andy Moonly stood up and said "That is a great idea, Wild Bill is 100 percent what we need here in this area to help us stop the rustlers. The truth of the matter is it would take too long for any one of them to come here. I also think forming a cattlemen's association is a great way to have eyes and ears open all the time lookin to stop these rustlers. I also think our Deputy Marshall here in Monark is the best tracker we have to lead us in chasing the rustlers."

Marilyn Milner stood up and asked, "What ramifications will come back to us, will we look like we are forming a vigilante organization and what can or will the law do to us on account of this?"

I stood up and said, "As sheriff in Monark, we have a right to form a cattlemen's association. If we can come together to fight off rustlers, then we look organized. We also look like we are working together, and this is more than can be said for other towns or areas."

Dave Milner stood up and said "we have a few things to vote on, number one – all in favor for forming a cattlemen's association raise your hand" – Dave looked over everyone seated and standing and said, "Passed."

If I had not seen this I would not have believed this – every body's hand, I mean one hundred percent of the people put their hand up – never before had Monark been this tightly wound together.

Dave Milner, the Mayor of Monark, said, "Number two – do we want Wild Bill Hickok to come in and help us, all in favor raise your hands." The mayor counted hands, then said, "Not in favor raise your hands," Dave counted hands and said "Majority vote not in favor for Wild Bill Hickok not come to Monark to help us with cattle rustlers. Number three – all in favor for the Deputy

Sheriff Alasdair Rumsel track the rustlers as long as it takes, all in favor raise your hands."

Again, if I had not seen this, I would never believe it, everybody here in this room has put their hands up.

Dave Milner said. "Passed; the Deputy Sheriff Alasdair will track the rustlers. There being no further business I declare this meeting closed."

Jim, Bob and Ken McKlay brothers were talking together when Dave walked up to them after the meeting was closed, Dave said "Sorry about that, I knew you wanted Wild Bill to come out to Monark to help run down the rustlers."

Bob McKlay said "That's OK, if things don't work out, I can still send a telegraph to Wild Bill and ask him his advice on certain things. You never know, he may just show up here one day, all on his own, traveling on his way to the Alaska Gold Rush."

Dave said "you know that's one person I would like to talk to, find out what he's up to and listen to his stories which I'm sure he has many, and they are probably all extremely exciting, the other person is Judge Roy Bean. Now, what do you all think about coming over to the saloon to talk about what has happened to-night, Arthur Fallas keeps coffee on for me because I don't like the taste of alcohol, for those that want a drink, they can."

Everybody thought this was a good idea, Andy & Mark Moonly, and their wives, Hubert and Esther Slinger, Jim and Bob McKlay, their wives and Ken McKlay, The Mayor, Dave Milner and his wife, Marilyn. The Sheriff Norman John and Deputy Sheriff Alasdair Rumsel's and his wife

Jacqueline all went to the Monark Brigantine Saloon for a drink of coffee or whiskey.

When everyone arrived at the saloon, Art Fallas even joined them and sat down with them, had coffee and said: "I hope you ladies don't object to the working girls in this saloon."

Andy and Mark Moonly moved all the tables and chairs around so that everybody could sit down in one group in a circle, have coffee or drinks, and still have a conversation.

Alasdair said, "Tomorrow will be the start of many busy days to come, and, I have a question, do any of you know about the new badge toting techniques invented in 1863, by Professor Paul-Jean Coulier of Val-de-Grace in Paris, France. In Paris he published his observations that (latent) fingerprints can be developed on paper by iodine fuming, explaining how to preserve such developed impressions and mentioning the potential for identifying suspects' fingerprints by use of a magnifying glass. We can sure use this when we start to round up these no good rustlers."

The Mayor's wife Marilyn said, "This new law and policing techniques are very interesting to me. Did you know the English were the first to begin using fingerprints in July 1858, when Sir William James Herschel, Chief Magistrate of the Hooghly district in Jungipoor, India, first used fingerprints on native contracts? On a whim, and without a thought toward personal identification, Herschel had Rajadhar Konai, a local businessman; make his hand print on a contract. The idea was merely to frighten him out of the thought of repudiating his signature. The native was very impressed, and Herschel made a habit of requiring palm prints on every contract. Later simply and only the right index and middle fingers required from the locals on every contract. Personal contact with the document, they believed, made the contract more binding than if they simply signed it. You see, the first wide-scale, modern-day use of fingerprints was predicated, not upon scientific evidence, but upon superstitious beliefs. Herschel collected fingerprints, and as his fingerprint collection grew, however, Herschel began to note that the inked impressions could, indeed, prove or disprove identity. While his experience with fingerprinting was admittedly limited, Sir William Herschel's private conviction that all fingerprints were unique to the individual, as well as the fingerprint was permanent throughout that individual's life; this inspired him to expand the fingerprint use."

Alasdair said "Marilyn, matter a fact, that, I did not know. In Scotland Policing, I think you would do very well."

Both Andy and Mark sat slack-jawed, they had no idea the schooling their little sister had on this topic.

Mark said, "Sis, is there anything else you are keeping from us or do we have to guess at what else you have a rope around and how much of an expert you are in such matters."

Marilyn said "All you need to do is dust off your shell belt and clean that ghastly cowboy necktie for the rustlers. As far as I know, horse and cow rustling are still a hanging offense in these parts, lynching, though it often refers to hanging, the word became a generic term for any form of execution without due process of law. Lynching's it seems that they occurred only sporadically before 1865, and was likely to be the result of "frontier justice" dispensed in areas where formal legal systems did not exist, Go Get'm Bro."

T he Sheriff, Deputy Sheriff, The mayor, Hubert Slinger, Bob – Jim – Ken McKlay, Andy, and Mark Moonly were all together in a meeting to decide when to start tracking the rustlers.

The Mayor asked, "Sheriff, when can Alasdair start the tracking and chasing the rustlers?"

"Alasdair, the Deputy Sheriff, can start tomorrow morning. As a matter a fact, as stated in the last meeting we had, Alasdair will be assigned to this job of bringin the rustlers to justice. He is not to show his face on the streets in Monark until he finished looking for and captured the cattle rustlers."

Andy Moonly said "Finally, we'll have some cattle rustling justice taken place, and we the cattlemen's association is finally safe. I just hope we can track these cattle thieves down. Sheriff, can we shoot the rustlers on sight if we catch them?"

"Yes, with the stipulation that the cattle rustlers caught, are without a shadow of a doubt, the rustlers we're looking to catch! He or they, you have to catch them in the act of taken the cattle and they cannot be the ones that purchased the cattle. Then and only then, you can string them up with a rope."

Hubert Said, "With the help of the Deputy Sheriff, who can track a gopher over a rock pile, we should have a pretty good chance of bringing these no good owl hoots to justice."

Mark Moonly said "count me in; I'm tired of these low-down, thieving, polecats, they're takin our beef away from us. I tried to count how many we're losing every year; I believe it's close to a total somewhere around the three hundred cows. We are just staying at a constant number in our cattle herd, not increasing or decreasing in large significant numbers. These low down owl hoots are taking most of our yearly profit, some years the same, some less, can't last much longer with the wages we have to pay out for all the hired hands and operating costs."

Jim McKlay said "I'm in, let's get down to brass tacks and bring these yahoo's in, and stop the thievery from happening to every rancher here in Monark and surrounding area. Time to have these cattle rustlers pay the fiddler, they that stole must pay for all the cows taken from the Monark area large and small Ranchers."

Alasdair said "yes, I agree, we'll track these no good varmints. One way or tuther, we'll have the no good jiggers either sitting up or lying across the saddle when we bring them in. I'll be ready at first light. I think we can all have breakfast at Fred's place when he opens up, so we can meet at first light, and discuss our plans and eat. We can do all this at the same time, and we'll all work together, nobody will be late."

Everyone thought this was a great idea they all said

their goodbyes to include, "see you tomorrow," and everyone left for their homes.

When Andy and Mark were riding towards their home, Andy said, "OK bro, now's the time, let's go get them. The time is now for the rustlers to pay the fiddler, and we'll be able to find out where all this beef is ending up and sold, maybe even get some of our beef back and put some coin back in our pockets."

Mark said, "These rustlers, they can't have a think bucket bigger than a little ole pea size and smaller than gophers think bucket, they must know somewhere, somehow, sometime, somebody will find out who they are and stop them."

Hubert Slinger, Jim – Bob – Ken McKlay were going to their homes, all four were riding the same way. All four men were happy and agreed that finally, something was going to be done about these rustlers and the loss of their beef.

Bob said, "You know, I do believe this is the ointment that killed the fly, these cattle rustlers are going to get the business end of my colt 45."

Jim Said, "yes! These nasty, thieving, slippery, slimy crooks are going to have their plans messed up, and we're going to be chasing these guys to the end of their time which will end up at the end of a rope or my gun."

Ken said "This is it boys when you want to catch a thief you must think like a thief, I'm going to get the gears in my think bucket working tonight, try to have some good idea's by tomorrow morning, I'm going to catch me a rustler. I'm going to give somebody a world of hurt, if I can have my way, I'll put one of the silver bullets from my shell belt into his think bucket."

At seven o'clock next morning when Fred opened the front door of his hash house, everyone was there in front of the eatery waiting for Fred.

As Fred opened the door, in his very hoarse and coarse voice which was almost a growl, he said, "Last night I built me a fire pit out back with a steel spit and all. Now I'll be able to roast chickens, turkeys, pigs and big slabs of beef roast on a spit for my various menus. I'm lookin forward to cookin using this, and I'll have a bigger menu for my eatery supporters."

When everyone was sitting down, Fred's wife came and took their orders. Most everyone asked for steak with flapjacks and coffee.

Waiting for the plates of food to come, Bob asked Alasdair "I heard you can trail a beetle across a rock pile, how do you do that?"

"Keep the heid, noo jist haud on."

Bob said, "whatever you said, what in blazes does that mean."

Alasdair chuckled and said, "OK, let me slow down and explain, keep the heid means stay calm, don't get upset and noo jist haud on means now just hold it and slow down."

Bob queried "Do all you in Scotland talk the same way."

The deputy marshal said "ye, or in your lingo, I Reckon."

All the people at the tables gave a chuckle, and the mood became a little friendlier.

Alasdair said, "ye slow down, don't lose ye head, look

at all ye see, understand all ye see, and most importantly, keep the heid noo jist haud on."

Bob said, "Marshall, I have no idea what he said can you explain what he just said."

"I sure can Bob, Alasdair said, slow down, don't lose your head, look closely at what you see, see what you look at, understand what you are looking at and most importantly keep your head and hold what you see and also important is slow down."

Alasdair said "When ye look at leaves on a tree or bush, look to see if any is pointing in other directions, then the majority of leaves hangin there, when ye look at the grass, look to see if any grass is bent over. When ye look at the hoof print in the dirt, look to see how deep and well-formed the print is, this will tell you how long ago the hoof print was made, also look for cow or horse droppings, the splatter will indicate the direction traveled. Then there is the number of owl hoots."

Jim McKlay said, "What about when someone uses a tree branch to drag over the trail to remove the horse and cow prints, how do you read that sign?"

Alasdair chuckled and said "This is a little bit harder. Now ye have to study the main ground in front where the trail was; ye have to look closely to see which way the small dirt, pebbles, and swirls go when ye don't see the swirls or pebbles go in the same direction, now ye looking at what ye don't see."

The breakfast food came and at the table everyone was quiet, there was no talking while eating. You would think the food was the best anybody had ever had, because the only sound was the knife and fork clicking and a clacking

on the plates as they cut the steak, eggs, and potatoes, and the sound of the fork is picking up the food.

After breakfast, Bob said "I sure am looking forward to watching you track these owl hoots, them that stole our cattle.

Hubert said, "excuse me for just a mite, I want to go see if my friend from down south has answered my telegraph."

Ken Said "Hubert, is there anybody you don't know?"

"Not many, at least not many people worth knowing."

Bob said, "What do you think Sheriff, when should we start this task of finding those no good polecat cattle rustlers?"

"I think we should mount up and ride as soon as Hubert gets back. We're all together in this and no one at any time is to be left behind. We are only as strong as the weakest rope, and by jiminy, there are no weak ropes in this group as long as I'm around."

Hubert came back from the telegraph office and said: "My friend Bill has not answered my telegraph yet."

Alasdair said, "Mount up, let's ride, we have a fair piece to go to the McKlay Ranch. Jim, I want for ye to tell me about 1 mile before where ye lost the tracks. Most important is you must point this area out to me so I can study the area."

Andy from the Four Diamonds Moonly Ranch said, "Finally, we're gonna look for those owl hoots that have been taken our cattle, at least if nothing else we'll be able to stop them from taken any more cattle.

After almost two hours of riding and Monark was behind them, the McKlay Ranch was in sight and to the right, the Curtshill School is to the left.

Alasdair said, "Jim, ye let me know when we are about the spot where ye lost the trail."

Jim said, "might as well start looking now, it is about 1 mile up to where the rustled McKlay cattle tracks from the Ranch, and it's also about 1 mile to where we lost the tracks of the cattle and horses."

Alasdair dismounted from his horse; he squatted down to look at the dirt and roadway as well as any trail tracks. Alasdair said, "Men, please stay mounted and don't move around, stay put as much as ye can." Alasdair looked this way, that way, laid on the ground and looked along the road. He walked left and looked, walked forward and looked, walked right and looked, he picked up a hand full of dirt and let it fall. Alasdair looked at how the pebbles landed, rolled and stopped on the surface of the ground.

Alasdair remounted and said, "OK, let's go to where you lost the tracks, Gie it laldy, Jim, can you let us know when we are at the place where the cattle trail was first lost."

They all started off at a slow pace, Alasdair said, "Ride on the grass, not on the trail this will help me follow the cow and horse tracks, and ride slow and easy, this will help to save the horses for a big run if needed."

When they arrived at the spot, Jim said, "Deputy, we are here at the spot where we lost the trail, look, here is the cold trail leading to this spot in the road then nothing, no more tracks."

Alasdair said, "Don't ye move, don't ye walk on this spot, don't ye mark this area up." He dismounted and looked closer, he squatted down and with his fingers found ridges left by the tree branch pulled along the road. He looked closer and found the ridges only went in one direction; this meant the tree branch was pulled in only one direction and was pulled only once over the cattle hoof prints. Then Alasdair remounted and sat in the saddle lookin for the ridges he had seen when he was squatting down; he found that these were too hard to see from sitting on top of the horse. Alasdair dismounted again, he took a pair of Indian moccasins out of his saddlebag and said "I'm going to have to walk to see the trail, Here Hubert, can you take my horse for me?" and he gave the reins to Hubert. Alasdair changed from his boots to the moccasins to walk in, and put his boots on the saddle, and tied them to the saddle horn.

When Alasdair was once more on the path that the tree branch had been pulled over, he could see the pattern left by the tree branch. OK, men follow behind me, here we go."

Ken said to no one in particular "Will you look at this; he has eyes of an eagle, now I know for sure he can follow a beetle over a rock pile.

Alasdair walked for what seemed to be 8 miles, occasionally he would squat down, check for ridges in the soil left by a tree branch and leaves, and then he would stand up and continue walking again.

At approximately 8 miles from where they started following the trail, Bob said "Look, unless I had seen this with my own eyes, I wouldn't believe it. You followed the trail we couldn't see, Alasdair, you have done the impossible. You have led us right to where the trail starts up again. Dang, nabbit Deputy, I'll talk to the Sheriff, and tell him that he is not in any way paying you enough, by gum, well done."

Hubert said, "I suggest that we follow this trail as close to Biggar as possible, then we cut off to the left and go into Biggar for supper, and I need to send a telegraph to my friend Bill again."

Bob, Jim and Ken McKlay thought this was a good idea; Andy Moonly said, "Wooo-eeeee, that's the best idea I've heard yet, I'm going be able to go to the theater tonight, I hear there is a traveling show in Biggar."

The Sheriff Norman John said, "Wow! I'm so hungry I could eat the southbound part of a northbound skunk, good idea, let's go to Biggar!"

Everyone agreed and started following the trail again.

Norman John dug into his saddle bag and came up with jerky for everyone, He said "here, eat this, this will help a little until we have supper at the hash house. Too bad the owner in Biggar doesn't cook as well as Fred in Monark."

As they followed the trail, at Oban the trail took a right turn and started to head towards the west.

Alasdair said, "Will Ye look at this, we can pick this up tomorrow morning here in Oban, let's go to Biggar for supper."

When they arrived in Biggar first, they went to the town well pump and washed the dust off their face, arms and hands. Then they all went to the hash house; the advertising sign said the meal tonight was a beef roast all cooked in gravy, potatoes cooked in a pot. Corn on the cob cooked with cream mixed in the water to help fatten the corn kernels, and it seems the corn kernels pick up the sweetness from the cream, and there was also a fresh loaf of bread on the table.

Everybody sat down to eat a big meal, all were talking in friendly terms with a dash of good humor on the side, and all were as hungry as a bear in springtime.

During the meal, there was a little conversation. However, the main topic discussed was tomorrow we start again after breakfast, and we all meet at Fred's hash house.

Alasdair said, "Everybody, I want you to listen up, you bring enough to camp out when we start following the cattle trail. Bring enough as nobody knows how long this will take to follow the cows to where ever they're being taken. Everybody will need a tent, or you sleep under the stars, blankets, bacon, eggs, coffee, potatoes, beans, canteens of water, maybe some dried meat and pack horse."

Next morning, everybody met at Fred's Place and had

breakfast together, after breakfast, all the men moved out to their horses.

Alasdair said "Is ye all ready to go as far as needed. We may even have to go all the way to that new small startup town; you know that new little town name of Calgras."

Hubert said, "I hear this is one very rough town, keep your eyes open and watch your friends back. The town started around a fort and all because of the liquor that sold to the Indians. Some trappers from the south of Calgras were comin up and killing the Assiniboine Indians, Upper Canada started a new sheriff's office, and they were sent to keep the peace in that new little town. Before the police came a fort was set up, and a town grew up around the fort, still dreadfully rough around the edges from what I hear."

Alasdair said, "Mount up, let's ride like the wind, we have some distance to go to get to Oban, and then follow the cattle trail west."

As they were riding and were coming near Oban, Andy said "Mark, remember when we were both kids, dad was milking the cow so we could have milk in the morning. Remember the stray cat that came into the barn area. Dad is sitting on his little three-legged stool. He had his head tucked in the hollow of the cow just in front of the left side hind leg and behind the stomach, the milk pail just below the utter."

Alasdair said, "look, here's the trail, leading straight west."

Mark burst out laughing and said, "Do I, you bet I do, I also remember that you picked up the cat and put it

on the back of the cow, then pulled its tail, the harder you pulled, the more the claws went into the back of the cow."

Andy laughed and said "I never knew a cow could arch it's back that high. When those claws of the cat went into the cows back, the cow let out a loud snorted bawling sound. The cow's, eyes went as big as saucers, and the cow arched her back up and down right fast as I remember. The cat's head was a bobbin up and down with the cow's back arching up and down. The cat hung on more tightly with all its claws, and the cat was still bouncing and moving about 1 foot up and down. The more the cow bounced, the more the cat hung on, the cat's eyes were wide open with its head bouncing up and down going side to side. It looked like the cat was lookin for a place to jump. Then the cat let out a long wild cat yowl. The cat scream surely did scare the cow which started to bounce up and down even more and faster. The cow with all four of its feet off the floor at one time. The milk pail went flying in one direction, the small three-legged stool in another direction and dad let out the loudest WHOA I ever heard. Then he seemed to fly straight back with an IIIEEEE sound landing on his back and his hat flying towards the door. Meanwhile, the cat is still holding on with all his claws, then it let out a wild bobcat shrill and took off with its tail straight back. He bolted for the barn door in the most frantic run I ever saw. Never did see that cat back here ever again after that. I'm thinking the cat never stopped running until it got to the next county."

Andy said, "I also remember the britches tanning with that willow branch that I received, couldn't sit down for a week."

All the men riding went into a fit of howling laughter, Bob, Jim and Ken almost fell off their horses, Hubert was bent over and issued the sound of hooo-hooo-hooo with laughter, and, Alasdair was laughing so hard he had tears in his eyes.

When all the laughter had died down, Hubert Said, "As I remember, you Moonly's had a pretty colorful upbringing."

Andy and Mark said in unison, "We lived on a farm, we had to make our fun, and nobody got hurt, and just maybe, we calmed down some of the farm animals while having fun."

Alasdair said, "Andy, Mark, is there nothing you boys are afraid of?"

Mark said, "I don't think we left anything out or undone, Andy and I tried most everything we could on the farm, this even included riding bulls and steers as well as unbroken horses."

Time went on, and Alasdair said "We've been riding for about three weeks and look, the trail is starting to angle down south a little. Look at the horse prints, one of the owl hoots, his horse has a shoe comin loose, the horse that made this set of tracks will be lame before the day is out."

Ken said, "These jiggers don't look after their horse's atoll, just maybe we could give them a lesson in horse care after we teach them rustling is not a good move looking for a job."

On the 25th day, they were still following the cattle trail, and the trail was still clear and able to see easily.

Alasdair said, "Look ye that, I see Calgras in the

distance, ye could be in the town by tonight, keep ye shell belt clean and make sure your 45 slides easily out of your holster, this could be very wild tonight."

Ken McKlay said, "Bring it on, I'm ready for you, I'm fighting mad, somebody has rustled our beef, and these no good cattle rustlers have more nerve than a throbbing tooth, and they got to be taught a lesson."

Both Jim and Bob made sure the Winchesters and the 45's were easily pulled from the leather holsters, and they also checked all guns loaded and ready for bear.

Bob said, "alright, you owl hoots, I'm ready for you, you're as good as mine, get ready to go down, you jiggers are going to draw your last breath if I find you."

Hubert said, "Lookit that town up ahead, I'm ready for a bath and then something to eat. I am tired of eating the things I cook. Time to eat somebody else's cookin for a change, it's only been 25 days, and I can't look at another Hard Tac Bun."

When the men from Monark arrived at the main street in Calgras, the street was quite active, the sound of the saloon piano keys plinking away was drifting out into the street, there were buckboards being pulled by horses on the road leading away from Fort Whoop-up. There were a few men what looked like gun slicks with their shell belt hanging low down below the waist on the right side, they all looked meaner than a she bear with a cub in tow.

Alasdair said, "what ye think, we go have a bath, then on to the hash house, we'll meet outside the bath house at seven tonight, that should let ye all have a bath and a shave."

Everyone thought this was the best idea anybody has ever had yet

At seven when they met, everybody was pink and squeaky clean from using the lye soap, they all met in front of the bathhouse, then they all walked together to the hash house to have supper.

The waiter came up and gave the menu to the table patrons to read.

Jim said, "Will you look at this; we even have a list of what the cookie can cook for us."

Ken said, "I think I'll have a steak, potatoes, peas and coffee with apple pie for desert."

Hubert said, "suits me fine, I'll have the same."

Everybody else agreed and ordered all the same.

When all the food was served, Jim said, "young feller, where is a good place to stay in this here town?"

The waiter said, "I don't recollect ever seeing you before, there's a place down the street called Ma's Place, I can't think of a better, safer or cleaner place to stay."

Hubert said, "Alright, that's a pretty good start, now where can we find the town's stock yards, which way do we go for them?"

The waiter replied, "That is a little bit harder to get to; you'll have to ride to the other side of the Elbow River to get to them corals."

After the waiter had left, Alasdair Said, "How about we meet in the lobby of Ma's Place at 7 in the morning, then we'll all come here to this hash house together for Breakfast."

8

After Supper, and while drinking coffee, Hubert said, "At the year ending 1860, the settling of the area south of Calgras, this changed the peaceful situation in this area. Traders began to come into this area and invade the hunting grounds of the Blackfeet Indians, which included the whole of the southern part of this area, south of the North West Territories and Red Deer Rivers. Large numbers of reckless traders entered this county and area, did as they pleased. They ruined the Indians with rot gut whiskey, built strong forts and established a reign of terror and murder. Whiskey was traded (to the great advantage of the trader) for buffalo hides, wolf pelts, and other skins. Goods to be exchanged for the furs were brought in without duty, and the whole trade was carried on in defiance of the laws of Canada and the country south of here. The Police were sent here to Calgras from Upper Canada to keep the peace and straighten the fur trade out."

When everyone arrived, they all met with the morning greetings and then sat down for breakfast. After giving their order for breakfast Alasdair Said, "Rustling gives a very handsome profit, in claims made against the Mexican government, for example, it was tallied that from 1859 through 1872 Mexican bandits stole 145,298 cows from the country south of here. When the Indians get hungry, they will steal horses and cows. The cow's innards found in the field of grass, and no other part of the animal can be found. Cow rustling is like a gauge marker as to how well the country is doing and how many people have jobs and how many people have a jingle in their pockets and with full bellies."

Breakfast came, and the table topic became lighter, Andy Moonly said, "Mark, do you remember when we were kids; we had this small horse, we made a harness out of small rope, tied the hoss to a piece of wood. The front of this wood shaped to ride up easy on top of the ground, and the flat wood shaped like a stone boat. There was a rope for us to hold on, you and I jumped on this stone boat, we never had any reins to the horse. We gave the horse a whack and hung on, and let the horse run where it wants. Well, that horse took off with a bound lickity split just like a bullet come out of a gun, it ran around the farm and barn area twice, then it took off even faster past the house towards the cow range area. The sound of the board draggin in the dirt skeared the hoss more, and it ran faster. Mom was lookin out the window when her two little boys flashed by the window on the old piece of wood swayin this way and that, and the horse's mane and tail were straight back, whoa! What a ride! If it weren't for grandpa, who said, "Can I try that," both of us would have had our britches tanned, again."

The group at the table laughed and snorted as Andy

was telling the story. Alasdair laughed and snorted so long, and hard coffee came through his nose. Then Alasdair started coughing and kept coughing until he could breathe again.

After breakfast the group of 7 crossed the river and rode up to the town's stock yards, they dismounted and walked over to where the office was and walked in.

Andy walked over to what looked to be the Segundo and said, "Good morning, my name is Andy Moonly. Meet my brother Mark Moonly; we own the Four Diamonds Ranch in Monark, North West Territories. Have you had cows come through here with the Four Diamonds Brand on them, and do you have any brands here that were made with what looks like a runin rod or a runin wire to change the brands?"

The man in the office replied, "Morning, the name is Jeff Dockerly, when we get the cows in here, brought in by someone I don't know, or they look shady, then we check very close. Otherwise, I just mark the brands down in the ledger book, when the cows come in for sale at these stockyards. The fact is, that the rustlers know the cattle country and are very good at roping, branding, and trailing a herd. A rustler only needs to buy a few cows, register a brand, and begin branding strays. Many cowboys had herds that increased so fast that some Ranchers refused to hire any hand that had stock of his own. If you write down your brands, I'll go through my ledger and see if any come up anything close to yours.

Andy Moonly wrote their name and brand down, then Jim McKlay, and finally Hubert Slinger wrote his name and brand down.

Hubert Said, "well, if you find any brands close to what we wrote, you can find us at Ma's place. Right now we are going over to see the Sheriff; we have a message for him from the Sheriff in Monark, it seems these two fellows knew each other from before, they went to school together. They were also good friends, and they also chummed around together as younguns."

When they had crossed over the river to go to the fort, they were just going into the fort when Daryl Mcfidgen had seen Alasdair.

Daryl said, "Alasdair you old Scottish tycoon, how are you and that lovely wife of yours doing. I haven't seen you or anybody from Monark for more than a dog's year. Can we get together tonight for supper, pull a cork and remember old times. Most important, why are you here? Ken, you old maverick, sure do miss having coffee with you, my old friend. I sure could use your marshaling skills here, how is my very good friend Norm doing?"

Alasdair told Daryl all about the rustlers and tracking the cows down here, and Daryl had explained he would stop at the stockyard, talk to Jeff Dockerly to see if he can help out any.

Alasdair and Daryl had said their goodbyes then the group started towards Ma's Place.

Ken said, "What do you think, we go to the saloon, have a whiskey and wait for Ma's Place to open up."

Everyone thought this was a great idea, can even get out of this heat.

Ken smiled a big smile and squeezed a wink out of his eye, and said, "Let me buy you guy's a whiskey, I have some jingle in my pocket, from looking after all them chickens, even if Jim and Bob do steal a chicken every once in a while."

Bob and Jim looked a little sheepish at this remark, and they wondered how he knew about the missing chickens?

Ken went up and bought a whiskey bottle and seven glasses for the group. On his return to the table, he noticed a lady with the finest and shiniest straw-colored hair, her face was an oval shape, and she had one of those smiles that seemed to be so incredible it would magnetize you and make your knees weak and wobbly. The problem, however, was her eyes were red-rimmed in color.

As Ken was sitting down, he heard the woman cry, wail and then she said loudly "NO, I Will Not!", he also heard the man with her, reach across and slap her in that tiny beak of hers.

Ken leaned a little closer to the other table and said loud enough for all to hear, "HEY TOUGH GUY! Where I come from, we don't raise a hand to our women folk, and we certainly don't raise a hand when they're crying and carrying on."

The other man at the table had a look of being a card player, the heels of his boots run down. Obviously, he's in the midst of some hard times, no excuse to slap a lady, Ken thought

The card shark said, "Where I'm from, we don't barge into other man's goings on."

Ken said, "You just might not want to raise your hand again. This could be your biggest problem you've ever grabbed hold of in all your life! As I see it, you are nothing but a big, fat, lethargic bully, picking on small defenceless women." Then he said with a sneer, "Oh your mama would be so proud of you, you two-bit cat beater."

The card shark said, "You look like a feller that has just come off the boat and purchased clothes so he can become a Saturday night cow nurse."

"HEY TOUGH GUY! I have been nursing cows longer than you been playing cards, and every one of them cows, have better manners than you do on your best day, and I've also been a sheriff and every one of them bad ones had better manners than you do right now."

The card shark pushed his chair back with a jump, his fingers just an inch away from his shell belt gun.

Ken's lips curled, showing his teeth, and Ken said, "Mister, I've been lifting cows and calf's for a living most of my life. You don't frighten me in the least, I've stared down cows and bears, and when I was a sheriff I even stared down the wrong end of a barrel of a gun a time or two, all you have is a plum loco way of looking at things. Let's face it, you just don't look good, and your stink is worse than any of the cows I've seen."

Alasdair said, "Gie him a skelpit lug, oh, I forgot, give him a slap on the ear."

Ken thought the card shark looked like a rattler had been thrown on the table between us.

Then the card shark said, "Stand up, I'm callin you out, I'll shoot you down like a dog that you are."

Ken stood up and faced the card shark, the card shark's hand twitched. Ken's hand blurred in movement, and magically the 45 appeared in Ken's hand. There was one loud roar, and the shining 45 bucked in Ken's hand. A bluish colored and acrid smell of gun smoke filled the air.

The card shark's legs buckled and gave way; he crumpled to the floor with a bullet hole between his eyes. The bullet hole was a perfect triangle with that third eye Ken had just made.

Daryl McFidgin came in and saw Ken still had the 45 in his hand and said: "Ken I'll have to take your gun for 24 hours. What's going on here, Ken? I've never known you to shoot anything but a snake or a skunk."

"Daryl, I know you are just doing your job. However, I was just shooting a snake that had raised its ugly head, and he had also raised a hand and struck this here lady in the beak." Ken gave Daryl his gun.

The Police Officer, Daryl said, "Anybody else see this, Hubert, Moonly brothers and the McKlay brothers all said "Yes, we have seen this, just like Ken said, the other fellow called Ken out, Ken was just standing up for the lady. You know Ken. He stands up for those that can't stand up for themselves"

Daryl said "Ok, thanks, I'll go make my report, you had better watch out. This fellow is bad clear through, and we were watching and waitin for him to start something, we even suspected he was rustling cattle in your area of the North West Territories area and running them here in Calgras. The cows and horses went for sale, purchased and herded across the border. Ken, best you be careful, this fellow's name was Jim Flades, he hung around with Tim McNainar and Jeff Schneiderson all known cattle rustlers, the other two may come lookin for you Ken."

"I'll be looking for them, and when I find them, I bring them to you, do you have any Dodgers on them, this will make it easier for me to spot them easily."

Hubert said, "Daryl, when will you know from the stockyards if our rustled cattle came through here."

Daryl said, "Tonight at the supper table I'll pass any info I find on to you and fill you in on everything else that I find out."

The lady rose from her seat; there was a faint pink color at the bottom of her nose where that fellow Jim had hit her in the face and nose area.

The lady said, "Afternoon, my name is Lily Malone, thank you for coming to my rescue. That dog Jim Flades had put the squeeze on me to pay him for protection, I said no, I didn't want or need protection, and you had seen that fracas when he hit me wanting protection money."

Ken said, "It is my pleasure to meet you, Miss Malone, my name is Ken McKlay, and you, dear lady, you do need some protecting; only because you are the prettiest gal I've ever seen from here in Boom Town. You, dear lady, are one I would definitely want to throw a lasso around and take home to meet my mom."

Lily said, "Ken you are very gallant, may I join you and your friends at this table."

Ken brought a chair over to the table for Lily, he put the chair down beside his, and he pulled the chair out for Lily to sit down, and then he pushed the chair in when she sat down.

Ken said, "Lily, these are my two brothers, Jim and Bob McKlay, Andy and Mark Moonly, Hubert Slinger and Alasdair Rumsel, gentlemen this is Miss Lily Malone."

Hubert said, "Lily, what do you do here in this wild west town of Calgras."

Lily said, "I'm a dance hall girl, even a girl has to

make a living, I've had schooling in law, but there is not one person out here that will take a woman on to work in a law office."

Andy and Mark were whispering back and forth, and then Andy said, "OK, Agreed! Lily will you come back to Monark with us when we go. We can sure use you in our business. You can represent us, we'll talk to Dave Milner, the Lawyer in Monark, and we'll have you work in Dave's office."

Ken said, "Boys, that's the best news I've heard all day, I'll be able to ride into Monark every day and see this good looking pretty lady Lily, ooh, I'm feeling a prickly chill go over my backbone, boys thank you for bringing this lady to Monark."

Hubert said, "Come on boys, let's go to the hash house and have the supper meal.

Everybody agreed and thought this was a good idea as they were starting to feel hungry again.

Ken said, "Lily, can I buy you a steak dinner with all the fixings."

Lily said, "Ken, I would be pleased to have dinner with you, and you Moonly Brothers, I would like to join you in Monark, then I'll be able to see much more of this tall gallant man."

Andy said, "Alright, that's settled, I'll send a telegram off to Dave Milner and let him know we have someone to help us look after our ranch dealings and all the legalities."

Lily said, "Excuse me for just a little bit, I have to let Johnny the bartender know I just quit and won't be back to work here in this Wild West Town."

As Lilly and the group of 7 were walking to the hash house, Hubert said, "Lily, where do you hail from."

Lily told Hubert, she was from that little town in North West Territories called Maple Ripples, down by the Border, not too many people in that little village, maybe 50 people, no bigger than a flyspeck on a map."

9

The Police officer Daryl McFidgen rode over to see Jeff Dockerly in the Stockyards.

Daryl said, "I see you've met my friends from my hometown area of Monark. What can you tell me about the different brands that have come through here? Are there any ranch brands that look like a running iron has been used or possibly used?"

Jeff Said, "There are a couple of brands that are questionable. The brands could have had a running iron sent over the brands to change them. The only way to be sure, we'll have to kill the animal, remove the hide, and look at the brand on the meat to see if the brand had changed."

Daryl said, "Jeff do you have any of those questionable brands on any cows in your stockyards, and if so, may we look at them, just so that we can get a better handle on this."

"As a matter a fact, I'm waitin for the trail boss to come here, take possession of the cows. The buyer has already been here and purchased all the beef that came into these stockyards."

"When can we go down and have a look at those critters."

"We have about ¾ of an hour, let me get my ledger, and we'll go down right now and give an eyeball, to those critters in the stockyards."

Daryl and Jeff climbed up on the stockyard fence to have a look at all the cows.

Daryl said, "Let me have a look at that ledger book."

Both Daryl and Jeff studied the brands in the ledger book very closely.

Daryl said, "Jeff, look at this, here is a brand that has two lines side by side. The angle line to make a Z looks like it was added later. The angle line is smaller in width and not as dark, plus the hair is grown out more on the two lines side by side – whose brand is this?"

Jeff Looked up the brand and said, "Would you look at that, this brand belongs to one of the Ranchers that just came in today to see me, belongs to Hubert Slinger."

Daryl said, "How many cows in this stockyard belong to Hubert."

"62 cows belong to Hubert."

"OK, now which brand do you see, that's close to you?"

"Here's one, "Jeff said, "Here is a Y with a box around it. Look real close, the left line is not as wide as the right side of the Y line, and the left Y color is not the same. The bottom of the Y is not the same color as the top left part of the Y; this looks like a running iron was used to alter the brand."

"Whose Brand is this, and how many cows are in the stockyard?"

Jeff Counted and said, "This brand belongs to the

McKlay Ranch in Monark, and there are 75 cows here in this pen."

Daryl said, "Ok, what's next and how many?"

"Look at this, four diamonds with a J on the front and an F on the back side. These cows were brought in by Jim Flades. Will you lookit this, the J and the F look like the letters were added later, and there are 90 cows here, they belong to the Moonly ranch.

Daryl thanked Jeff, then Daryl went off to have supper with Ken and the boys from Monark. When Daryl met with Lily and the boys, he brought a chair over and sat down. He could not, however, put a chair in between Ken and Lily; they were as tight as the hair on a dog's back.

Daryl said to Ken, the fellow you shot was a very bad hombre. He was a cattle rustling ring leader. "Then he said to Hubert, "I have found 62 cows that belong to you." He said to the Moonly brothers, "Andy and Mark I have found 90 cows for you." He said to the McKlay brothers "Jim and Bob I have found 75 cows for you. Gentlemen, these brands of yours, Jeff and I can see the brand has been changed. In the morning take your 75 cows home. Ken, you come by in the morning and pick up your shooter. Before you ask, the person who bought these cows will face a charge of buying stolen property."

Then he smiled at Ken and said, "I see you two have met, I was going to introduce you two lost souls together. Now, most important, tell me, how is my old friend Norm doing, is that old night crawler still keeping the peace in Monark?"

Both Jim and Bob said, "Daryl, you are being missed enormously by Norm in Monark. Norm, he sure does miss having breakfast with you, and there are times he looks like a heifer lost her calf. He walks around not thinking straight, some days he can't concentrate and other days he just plain ornery. Oh, he sure does miss his best friend!"

Hubert said, "Maybe we can convince Norm to take some time off from the sheriff's duties. Come down here to Calgras, never know, he just might like it here and stay. On the other hand, 21 of August in 14 1/2 months, the package Norm ordered from that mail order bride page in the catalog arrives in Monark, and from what I hear, she's a looker alright."

Andy said, "Daryl, how are you doing, are they keeping you busy or is there too much work here for you. Have you been able to slow down the Black Feet Indian killing? The whiskey trading, were you able to put a stop to the whiskey trading or at least control or slow down that trading?"

You sure don't beat around the bush, do you? I sure could use Norm's help here; I am too busy. Alright, let's see, there are times we are busier than a person taking honey from a bee hive, with all the traders, cattle buyers and just plain bad jiggers that come up here to Calgras. Yes, after a time and a lot of saddle work we were able to stop the Indian killing and serve justice to those that make the killing. The whiskey trade is another story, the good thing, however, is that we were able to stop the whiskey trading on the Indians doorstep. Yes, there is so much work here for a sheriff, Norm could come here and become a territory sheriff with no problems, his past performance speaks loudly. There would also be a pay increase, and he has a good reputation as sheriff in Monark. When you get back to Monark, can you ask Norm if he would consider comin to Calgras and work as a Territory Sheriff?"

The dinner orders taken for the evening meal; everyone was in a gracious mood, and, if you looked closely, it would seem Ken and Lily were sitting a mite closer together than ever.

Mark said, "Lookit this, Lily and Ken – you couldn't put a zig zag cigarette paper between the two. How does that go, something about two lost souls find each other and become stronger and tighter or something like that, as I see it, couldn't happen to a better person. Finally, Ken can howl at the moon and chase a skirt."

As the supper meal was placed on the table Hubert said, "How do you feel about we start back in two days, let's say we start about 10:00 O'clock in two days."

Ken said, "I'll stop by the Blacksmith shop and buy one of those Prairie Schooners, load it up and I can also take all of Lily's suitcases and trunks in the wagon."

"Ken," Hubert Said, "I noticed you pulled the lady's chair out every time for Lily to sit down, how gallant of you, and I'm sure Lily likes it. Also, you two make a very good lookin couple."

Jim said, "That is a great idea little brother, buy a wagon, we can even buy a few odds and ends while we're here and take back to our wives as a gift."

Bob agreed and said "I would sure like to buy some of that new material they have here so I can give to my wife. She can put the material up on the window, I heard somebody here call it a curtain, and I would also like to buy my wife a new dress, she hasn't had a new dress in over two years."

Jim, Hubert, the Moonly Brothers and Alasdair agreed and thought they would also like to buy a new dress for their wives, this being a big city and all.

Just as the supper meal was finishing Daryl said: "Gentlemen, I'll have to leave you now, see you in the morning."

Hubert said "Daryl, I heard you had some bad luck with your horses dying off, I have a string of pretty good horse flesh, I can bring them down here for you. I have also asked the animal doctor to look into as to why your horses have died."

"I'll pass that on to Inspector Brisebois."

Bob said, "Daryl, we'll be by your office about 9 in the morning after breakfast, we'll say our good bye's and Ken can pick up his 45, we want to be on the trail by 10, the day after tomorrow."

Daryl said, "I'll be here at 7:30 in the morning to have breakfast with you all, and then we can all say our goodbyes."

The next morning everybody was up bright and early, getting ready to pack and load the wagon ready to move out the next morning.

At breakfast, they all said their good bye's and Lily said, "Daryl, you and the rest of the constabulary, thank you for everything you have done for me, including making sure I was as safe as could be."

After Breakfast, Ken went to look for a prairie schooner; he found a wagon that the people had just finished building. They haggled the price and finally settled on 100 dollars for the wagon, horses included.

Ken brought the wagon around to the hotel, he carried

the luggage down for Lily and put the trunks and carpet bags in the prairie schooner.

Hubert, Andy, Mark, Bob, Jim, Ken, and Alasdair all put their carpet bags in the prairie schooner.

All day Ken and Lily were together, walking close as can be, they were talking in such low tones nobody else could understand or make out what they were saying.

Ken and Lily went to the Mercantile to buy pans to cook the meals in and also replenish the food, coffee, and water needed for the trip back to Monark.

After the wagon had been filled with the trunks, carpetbags, and presents, Andy said "Let's all go down to the stockyards and let the operator know we'll take the cattle tomorrow morning and start the trail back to Monark, North West Territories, we start right after breakfast.

Jim went down to the hash house owner and asked if he would open early for everyone in his group to have breakfast at 6:00 in the morning, the owner agreed, and Jim departed and explained to everyone that there would be an early breakfast served at 6:00 in the morning.

10

T he next morning, the hash house opened at six in the morning as requested for the group of 7 and Lilly to have an early breakfast.

During breakfast, Hubert said: "Ken and Lily, they will drive the wagon, look after cookin, keep the water canteens full, cleanup after meals, wash and dry all the dishes, pots, and pans, etc."

"Mark, can you lead the cow herd?" – Mark Agreed

"Andy, can you ride left flank?" – Andy Agreed

"Alasdair, can you ride right flank?" – Alasdair agreed

"Jim and Bob, can you ride left and right rear flanks?" Jim and Bob agreed

"I'll do the pushing and watch for stray's Jim and Bob miss bringing back to the herd."

By 7:30 everybody finished breakfast.

Lily said, "I'll do the cooking best I can on the trip to Monark."

Everybody had no complaints, and Bob said, "Wish you would do all the cooking, we tried Ken's cookin once, even the dog wouldn't eat it. In fact, when I think back, the dog took it away and buried it, so no one in the group could get sick on it."

Hubert laughed with his hooo-hooo-hooo, then said, "Lily, thank you for cookin, it'll save the dog from dyin."

Ken and Lily went to get the wagon and horses and make sure everything is tucked away in the wagon, and all the items placed near the back of the wagon would not fall out or get left behind.

The rest of the group went to get the cattle and start this cattle drive back to Monark.

The group of 6 gathered all the cattle at the stockyards and started to move the herd on the trail back to Monark.

Bob said to the rest of the group "What about Ken and Lily?"

Hubert said, "When they get everything tied down, they'll be on their way, and they'll catch up to us further down the trail."

Lily and Ken had the wagon packed, and they started to drive the horses and wagon on the trip, about a half hour after the herd had left the town area. Lily was seated next to Ken, as a matter a fact; Lily was so close, there was no daylight showing between them.

Lily said to Ken, "I bought a new type of stove, and packed it in the wagon. This new stove is one that can be used while the wagon is being hauled across the trail. It is shaped like a large flat bowl with legs attached to the bottom to hold it up. The bowl is about eight inches high with a grill across the top. Now I would like to get in the back and get the stove ready, and then I would like to start making dinner. This dinner I plan, I picked up from a couple from Germany it's called Kleisel and Grebbon.

The name means potato dumpling and bacon. I'll start by lighting the stove, peel the jackets off the potatoes in the back, mash the raw potatoes and add some flour, make balls out of the mashed potatoes, then cook these in water; I'll also cut bacon into cubes and cook the bacon. When the potatoes are done, I'll add these to the bacon, can even add an onion to give taste."

Ken thought this was a good idea and said, "Lilly, you sure will get on the good side of all the men by having dinner ready when we stop at dinner time, oh they will think the sun will rise and set on you."

Three hours later the group and cattle stopped for dinner. When Lily started handing out the plates, cup, knife, fork, fresh bread and a homemade dish of food the men were all standing around slack jawed, mouth open and the jaw is not closing and mouth watering from the food aroma.

Finally, Hubert said, "Girlie what have you done here, you've been making dinner while the wagon is moving, I never, in all my days, I never saw or heard of that being done before."

Lily explained and said, "There was a new type of stove shipped into Calgras from down south, from the city called Chicago."

When the group started eating, everyone stopped, looked at each other and Bob said, "Ken will be getting a gal that is not only a looker she can also cook too. She'll be a great person to have with us on this trail ride back home. I only hope I don't gain any weight before I get home to my wife, she'll be a fretten, where have I been, to eat this well and gain weight."

On the 13th day, as they were getting close to the North West Territories River, Lily looked up and seen all the Indians in a long line on the horizon lookin at the cattle and the wagon train.

Lily said, "Ken, I've never seen this many Indians at one time, do you think we'll be OK?"

"These Indians are Blackfeet; the Indian chief is the one with the biggest headdress on his head, and, the chief's name is Navarone Stand With A Fist."

Ken called Hubert, Jim, and Bob over to let them know what Lily and he had seen.

Hubert said, "I've met Chief Navarone Stand With A Fist a few times before when I was going on a trip to buy cows and another time when I went buffalo huntin. I saved his life one time when we were hunting buffalo, he is a good leader, but he does not take well to lyin. I have always been honest to the Indian Chief Navarone Stand With A Fist, and I have always shown him respect."

Jim said, "Looks like he's coming down to parley with us, guess we'll find out what he wants soon enough."

When Chief Navarone Stand With A Fist reached the group, he stopped, and the six Indians with him stayed back behind about four feet.

Hubert Raised his arm up and swung his arm from left to right and said to Chief Navarone Stand With A Fist: "Ponokasisaahta Nii Sita pi miko-ew pikuni inuk'suk."

"My friend Hubert, are you well, do you have many lodges."

"Yes, my friend Chief Navarone Stand With A Fist, I have good lodges and many people in my lodge, How is your lodge, how are your wife and your children?"

Chief Navarone Stand With A Fist said, "My friend Hubert, my lodge is weak, my wife is hungry and my children not enough to eat."

"My friend Chief Navarone Stand With A Fist, I can help your lodge, I will give you 10 of my cows, for you and your lodges. Everybody will have strength again. You are Chief of many lodges, and you need to feed your lodges, in 10 days if you send 20 of your Braves to my ranch, I'll give them work lookin after my cattle, I'll give them 15 cows to bring back to you and your lodges."

"My friend Hubert, thank you for your help, someday you and I can go hunting buffalo together again, then we will smoke the pipe all day, you always have respect for my lodge."

Ken brought up ten cows cut out from the herd and said, "Hubert, here are three cows cut from each ranch and four from yours."

"Chief Navarone Stand With A Fist, here are the cattle for your entire lodges. This gift is from all of us, the McKlay Ranch, the Moonly Ranch and from my ranch. I hope you live a long life, my friend, next time we meet; we will smoke the peace pipe and remember good days with many buffalo running."

Chief Navarone Stand With A Fist raised his arm and signaled to the rest of the Indians that gathered on the hillside about one-quarter mile away, the Indian bucks close by the chief gathered the cows, they drove the cattle to the group of people on the hillside.

Bob said, "Hubert, what was that you said to the Indian."

"Well, this is how it works. First, he is not just the

Indian; he is Chief Navarone Stand With A Fist. Second, you have to pay a compliment; then you ask how all his lodges or all his houses are. Then you ask about his wife and children. This is what I said first, Ponokasisaahta niitsitapi miko-ew pikuni inuk'suk. Ponokasisaahta that means the territory between Calgras and North West Territories River. Niitsitapi means original people. Miko-ew means a good fighter and stained with blood, pikuni means largest group and inuk'suk means the humans, what I said to him was, chief of the land between Calgras and North West Territories River, the largest group of fighters stained with blood."

All the men shook their heads, wondering how Hubert had ever been schooled in all this.

Bob said, "Where did you come in contact with these Indians to learn all this?"

"When I was hunting buffalo, I ran into the Indian hunting party and Chief Navarone Stand With A Fist, they were also hunting Buffalo, when the hunt was over they had invited me to their camp for dinner, right hospitable they were, they looked after me very well that night. Ever since, whenever I meet Chief Navarone Stand With A Fist, and we will say hello to each other. We also use and show respect with each other, and, we call each other friend."

Andy said, "Let's get these cows moving, we've been on the trail for 13 days, and we're only halfway there."

Hubert agreed and said, "Get Them Doggies Movin Haaa!"

Lily and Ken cleaned up the camp and put things away in the wagon. Then they climbed up on the seat and sat so close together again; you could not see daylight between them.

Ken gave the reins a quick jerk, he made the reins slap the backs of the horses, and he let out a loud "HAAAAH! Get Up There You Nags!" He started the wagon moving to catch up to the herd.

Lily said, "I'll start making supper, skin the jackets off the potatoes and cook some steaks to have with coffee tonight. We have to finish the steaks before the meat goes bad."

Ken said "that was one good idea you had, you bought that new type of stove, now all the men now think they cannot do without you, as a matter a fact, I most of all cannot do without you. Lily, I have this feeling about you, I cannot live without you, I feel sick when I cannot see you, I have this funny feeling in my stomach when I am beside you, sometimes I feel hot, and sometimes I feel cold, sometimes I can't think straight. I don't know how I managed so long without you. Lily, will you marry me, we can be hitched next year in Monark."

"Oh Ken, I have been feeling the same way, and I didn't know how to tell you, it feels like you have taken out my innards, twist them up in a tight ball, and then you put them back inside of me. I have this tight pain in my stomach when I can not see you. Yes, I will marry you."

"Now we'll have to tell my brothers and their families, Hubert and the Moonly brothers, and when we get to Monark, I can tell my friend Norman John he's the sheriff in Monark, I can tell him all about you."

"Ken, there is so much I'll have to learn, about you, about the farm, about Monark."

"Don't you worry that pretty little head of yours, there'll be enough time for that and everybody at the Ranch will help you, we are not only a family, we are also friends."

"Ken, where can we build a house for us?"

"The McKlay Ranch is large, we can build where ever you want to park that pretty little head and curvaceous body of yours, or and preferably we can live in the main house where I live now. Lily, I'm starting to feel excited, marrying a beautiful lady, when I look at you I see about one thousand diamonds in your eyes, a glittering and a gleaming when you smile, you are without a doubt very beautiful."

"Ken, how I ever got so lucky to meet you I'll never know. I feel my whole world is starting to expand and will near to explode."

"Lily, your world has just started to expand, you wait and see I expect your eyes will go big as saucers when we reach our ranch."

When the boys stopped the cattle drive for the night Lily, and Ken told the group about their wedding plans.

Andy said, "I thought I had seen you two up there on that seat a sparkin, YAHOO! We're goin to have us a wing-ding of a party comin up; that'll be a shindig to remember."

Mark said, "You two are a goin ta have a good send off to your ranch when were done."

Bob said, "Little brother, I have been watching you these past few days, and you are growing up faster than I can keep up with you, I'm thinking our family is growing bigger again, and this one will fit in like a hand in a glove."

Jim said, "Little brother, you are starting to fill some pretty big shoes, I'm watching you, you are doing the right thing, this little filly will keep you in line, and we, that is all of us will help her."

Hubert said, "Girlie, you are biting off a pretty big bite. If you ever need help or you need somebody in your corner, I'm there for you. I've been a watchin you, I like what I see, and you carry yourself very well, I'm proud to know you."

Ken said, "Garsh, you guys are going to make a feller turn a red color if I didn't know better, I'm thinking you like her better than me, thank you for all your help and support."

The rest of the thirteen days were uneventful. However, Lily and Ken sat even closer on the wagon seat. At times it looked like Lily was sitting on Ken's lap, and every once in a while one of the boys would ride back to the wagon and say; "Tut-tut-tut, you two have to sit a little further apart than that. What would mom say if she saw you like that? You can't sit that close, not until after the Parson's has his say."

11

When the trail drive had arrived near the Slinger Ranch, the cows were separated, and the Slinger ranch hands drove the cattle to the rest of the Slinger cattle herd.

Hubert Said his goodbyes, and a thank you for everything the men had done to help him out on the cattle drive," he also reiterated, "Ken and Lily, you send the wife and I an invite to the wedding, we'll be there, that is a promise."

The McKlay Ranch hands were notified, the cows are coming home, and they had also had ridden toward the Slinger Ranch to meet the cattle drive, to help drive the cattle to the McKlay Ranch, and further if required.

When the cattle were deposited with the rest of the McKlay cattle herd, Bob said: "We'll help you Moonly's take your cattle to your ranch."

When the Moonly ranch hands had pointed the cattle towards the Moonly cattle herd, Andy said, "Bob, would you and your hands like to stay for supper here, I'll get the cook to lay on a feed bag for everyone here."

"No thanks, driving this herd we still have a far

distance to go before we get back home yet, and there is little light left that we can use in checking the cattle on the drive home. Can we make this meal in say in a week's time? We can plan a lunch, our family, and Ranch Hands together with your family and Ranch Hands."

That sounds like this could be a great time to have a wing ding, good idea, alright, let's do that next week, I'll get the cook to roast a cow at the pit in the garden, also please make sure Ken and Lily make it out for this."

Jim and Bob said their goodbye's and everyone left to go back to the McKlay Ranch.

Just after the McKlay Ranch group left, one of the Moonly Ranch Hands came in with a fellow all beat up. Both eyes were black and blue, both his arms tied behind his back. It looked like his back had been strafed with a cat of nine tails, the whip marks were cut deep in his back.

The ranch hand said to Andy, "Boss; I found this fellow and four others trying to take cattle off our ranch land. The other four got away, looks like we got us a rustler. I know what I would like to do to him, Boss, what would you suggest?"

Andy said, "Art, tell me everything that has taken place out there."

"Boss, we rounded the slew on the east pasture, you know the one with the bunch of trees grown around that south water hole. We saw these five fellows; I'm a thinkin their think bucket is smaller than a Gophers think bucket. They were makin a cow herd and started to drive the herd out of the slew area. They up and put their 45 in their hands, there were many bullets a flyin overhead, and these bullets sounded like angry bees a comin at us. Even put

90

three holes in my new hat, so we up with our Winchester's and let them have it, you know the new ones you gave us. That skeared them out of the thought of taken your cows. The ones that could ride well, they took off like a skeared rabbit. This one, we caught in an ambush, we taught him the right from wrong in stealin, then we trust him up like a chicken ready to cook and brought him here to you."

"I have just the answer, tie him up in the barn. Tomorrow I'll go to town and send a telegram to my friend, Judge Roy Bean. We all know what will happen there, and the judge will take care of this owl hoot. We won't be losing any more cattle by this thief, pretty hard to steal bovines when you're did."

Mark said "As a matter a fact, when there is a question about the innocents of a fellow because the fellow says he didn't do it. The Judge was known to kill the cow in question, he then had the hide removed and looked at the color of the meat. If the color of the meat is not the same color on the whole brand, you can see the difference between fresh and old brand marks, well the Judge had the fellow taken out to the hangin tree immediately. No questions asked, no parlayin and no repeals, he was hanged on the spot, the judge hates lyin almost as much as stealin."

Andy said, "I can't abide any more stealin, the next one we find tryin to rustle our cattle, we hang him on the spot, in the North pasture there is a sturdy tree, and I have a rope with their name on it."

"yes boss, we shore can do that."

"Art, you and brownie, I want you to listen close on this. Tomorrow you two will escort this owl hoot down south and give this man to Judge Roy Bean. I'll send a telegraph to my old friend and let him know you're bringin this rustler to him. Also, do not be tardy, do not hang around down there, do not stop in the judge's town for a beer or play poker. Soon as you drop this man off the judge will want to ask you questions and ask how I am. Soon as you're finished, you high-tail it out of there like there was a fire in your britches. I don't want to have to come down there to pick you up out of the judge's jail."

"Yes boss, we won't dilly dally, we won't be tardy, and we won't hang around doin nothin, we want to come back in time to see the package come in on the stage.

The next morning Art and Brownie started off with their captive with directions from Andy.

Andy went to Monark to send a telegraph to Judge Roy Bean located West of the Pecos.

"Good mornin Judge STOP. Hope you and the misses are good STOP. Haven't spoken to you in a while STOP. Sending three people to you STOP. Art and Brownie my ranch hands STOP. They will escort cow rustler STOP. Cow rustler was caught in the act taken cows by these two cowhands STOP. These two saddle pounders are my best cowhands STOP. Please say hi to the misses from myself, and my misses STOP. Your friend Andy Moonly

Andy said to the telegraph operator "I have a few chores to do in town, I'll be back later for the reply, and before you say anything, I know the judge will send a reply."

Andy went to Fred's place and had a bite to munch on; he was feeling hungry. Fred sure does know how makin that raisin pie becomes so palatable."

Andy thought, "I still have to see the smithy and my wife Bonnie asked me to check with the sheriff on the day the package is supposed to arrive on the stage. I can't forget to go to the mercantile and pick up the new dress Bonnie ordered all the way from Saint Louis.

The chores in town done, Andy walked over to the telegraph office and checked any messages.

The operator said "here's your answer, I'm plum impressed, I shore didn't think this would have a reply, how did you know?" and the operator gave Andy the telegraph answer.

"I've been friends with Judge Roy Bean for over ten years. You see I saved his life one time way back; this Yahoo came down the street waving his shooter at the judge. He was tellin the Judge him how and where he was going to shoot the judge. I just walked up behind the Yahoo, knocked his hat off, gave this galoot a solid right to the jaw, when he turned around. Well, down he went like a big bag of spuds, ever since then the Judge thinks I'm a pretty good fellow."

Andy read the note, "Andy, my good friend always good to hear from you STOP. Yes, the wife is good STOP. Thank you for sending the guilty owl hoot to me STOP. I'll take care of business when your riders show up STOP. I have a place in boot hill for him STOP. I still think you should come work for me and help clean up this area STOP. Say hi to Bonnie, and I send her my best STOP. Say howdy to my friend Ken McKlay STOP. Next, to you, he is the best sheriff I ever had STOP. Your friend Judge Roy Bean."

Andy wrote out a reply to the judge and gave it to the

telegraph operator, the operator read the note and said, "Are you sure you want to send this?"

"You bet I do; I wouldn't ask if'n I didn't want it sent."

The operator sent the telegraph, "Thank you Judge for looking after the problem for me STOP. If'n I ever get tired of chasing cows, I'll send you a telegraph asking for a job STOP. Somebody needs to look after your back side ha ha STOP. I will tell Ken you miss his help STOP. Thanks again, your friend Andy Moonly

When Andy arrived back at the Moonly Ranch, his wife Bonnie met him at the corrals and said: "OK, let me have the package from the mercantile, I know you have it, and I know it'll look good."

Andy gave her the package all wrapped up in heavy brown paper with the shop logo on the paper. Bonnie let out a squeal of delight and ran to the house to open the package she had just received.

Andy unsaddled his horse, put the saddle on the top cross pole and put the blanket on the saddle with the horse hair up so that the blanket will dry; then Andy walked to the house.

When Andy walked in the door, Bonnie yelled down: "Just a minute Andy, I have just about finished dressing, can you sit and wait for me?"

Andy said loud enough for Bonnie to hear: "Yes, I'll be in the parlor."

When Bonnie came down and walked into the parlor, Andy let out a loud, long whistle and a very fast rush of air with a wooo weee! Then Andy said, "You look purdier than a speckled puppy. This cream colored dress with a pink bow at the small of you back, OH my this looks good! The dress hugs every curve shows off all your flattering and vivacious curves. This dress will make every man whistle and drool when they see you. I am shorely impressed; you shore outdone yourself again." Then he winked and said, "I'll have to shoot every man jack that looks at you, so no one will try to take you home, and away from me."

Bonnie giggled, she gave Andy a poke in the ribs and said, "Oh you."

Andy said, "You will be the best-dressed lady on the twenty-first in the month of August when the package comes in for Norman John. Oh, by the way, Judge Roy Bean says hello and sends you his best."

"That old rascal, how is he doing, is he still the law west of the Pecos?"

"As a matter a fact, he is still the law, he even asked if I would go back down there to help him clean up the west, you never know, I won't say no just yet, and he even asked to say hello to Ken McKlay. Some day you and I can go down, you can have a holiday and visit with the Judge and his wife, and I can do some sheriff duties for the judge."

"Andy, we have not had a dance in a long time. After the package arrives, what do you think, how about we have a shindig? One to celebrate the package arrival. We can have a calf on a spit and all the fixings. Maybe we can ask Fred to come here and cook for us, that will let the Cookin staff join us in the festivities. We can ask the sheriff, Dave Milner and his wife Marilyn, McKlay Ranch and staff, Slinger Ranch and staff, and all of our ranch hands join us as well. The Parson can come to our ranch. Here he can marry Norm and his fiancée, Ken, and Lily. Oooeee this will be a shindig to remember."

"Bonnie, that is a great idea; this will be the biggest shindig since we got hitched."

Next morning Art and Brownie started off, escorting the cow rustler to Judge Roy Bean, Art said: "what is your name so I can call you something instead of rustler or gopher size think bucket, what is your moniker?

"I am William Jones of Wyoming, I shorley know I done wrong, and I shore don't want to go see Judge Roy Bean, he's one mean hanging Judge with no leniency."

"William, I'll tell you truly, the Judge, and Andy are good friends, you shore picked on the wrong brand this time to take something that ain't yours."

"I remember some time back; I was a saddle pounder, driven herds, don't make much money as a saddle pounder. The draw of makin easy money, taken others cows, this gives me more jingle in my pocket. But to tell you the truth, if I could do this over again, I shore would do it differently and I would do it right. I would go as straight as the crow flies, and I would keep others straight too if I could."

Art said, "Tell you what, William, next town we get to, I send a telegram to Andy, see if he'll say a good word to Judge Bean for you. Just maybe that will help some, and here's the but, the but is Andy and Mark are the best bosses I ever had, and I never want them to look bad. I ever hear of you takin something, not yours, if I hear you make them look bad, I'm comin after you myself. You'll be brought back, a lyin over a horse, not ridin or sitting tall in the saddle, no matter to me."

"Art, you do that for me, I'll ask Andy if I can work for him, and I'll pay all the ranchers for the cows I took."

12

When Art, Brownie, and William reached Regina, Art went over to the telegraph office, and he wrote a telegram. Moonly ranch Monark STOP. The man said he wants to work STOP. He wants to pay the bill for the cows took STOP. Can you telegraph judge and put in good word STOP. Will hear from judge one way or another when we arrive STOP. Art

Art came out of the telegraph office and said, "That's done. Now we'll find out the answer from the judge when we see him."

William said, "Art, I shore want to thank you fir what you done, I'll not let you down if I get out of this predicament I'm in, you'll see, I'll make Andy and Mark proud."

"William, I placed myself on the line for you, I put myself responsible, you fail then I fail, and I will not fail. Like I said before, you fail then I will bring you back laid over a saddle, no exceptions."

"I won't let you down Art; I'm beholden to you if I get out of this."

Brownie said, "Young feller, you let my friend Art

down, I'll be helpin Art, and we both come a lookin for you."

"You two not only work together, but you also look after each other. That's something I've been missing all these years, good friendship. I think if I met you in my early years, I would never have chosen to turn out this way. Now I want to go straight and make amends."

Art said, "We have a pile of miles to go, let's ride hard and put some miles behind us because I shore want to be back at Monark, before the twenty-first of August when the stagecoach comes in. I am excited, and I want to see that package."

Andy and Bonnie were making plans to have a cow cooked on the spit on the twenty-second of August. They sent out invitations to Ken McKlay and Lily saying, "The Moonly Ranch would pay for the Parson on the twenty-second of August. There will be a cow in the cookin pit to feed the Slinger Ranch, the McKlay Ranch and all their cowhands as well as the Sheriff and his new guest, the Deputy Sheriff, and his wife. Bill Moonly with his fiddle, Lance John with his squeeze box, and Art Fallas the saloon owner and his pie-ani., Dave Milner and his wife, Dave to call the dance, and also asked if Fred would cook the meal for them.

Bonnie said, "This is shaping up to be a pretty good foot-stomping party at our ranch."

Fred sent back the note, and he replied, "I would be pleased and proud to cook for you for that shindig on the 22nd of August."

The saloon owner Art sent word back, "Alright! I'll be there; I'll bring and play my pie-anie."

Bill replied with a nod "yes, lookin forward to the twenty-second of August, should be a good shindig."

The Sheriff Norman John sent a reply back which stated: "Thank you for thinking of my new guest and I, yes, we will be there, and lookin forward to the date and I'm glad the Parson is comin."

Hubert Slinger wrote back and said, "You are doing a great thing for Norm and his guest as well as Ken and Lilly, yes, my wife and I as well as the cowhands will be there."

Jim McKlay sent a note back to the Moonly Ranch, which said, "Count on it, we'll be there, all the McKlay men, their wives Ken and Lilly, as well as all our ranch hands, we will be there."

When Andy had received all the invitations back, there was only two months and twenty-five days left until the twenty-first of August 1875, and he said: "Bonnie, this will be the biggest, busiest and noisiest shindig that this area and the town of Monark has ever seen, bar none."

A couple of days after the seventh of June George Crossley rode over to the Moonly Ranch, he walked up to the front door and knocked. Andy came to the door and said "Hello George, please come in, what can I do for you?

"I came here to offer my services to help Fred when he cooks that cow on the cookin-spit, I've been friends with Fred, for a few years, and if it's OK with you I'll offer to help Fred."

"That's a swell idea, I'm a thinkin that Fred, would welcome the help, but you must remember, Fred, is the boss out here when the cookin is goin on."

"Thank you, Mister Moonly; I'll go see Fred right

away and let him know, bye for now and see you on the twenty-second of August.

George shook hands with Andy, and George walked out of the house and closed the door. He then went to his horse, climbed on up into the saddle and headed out of the yard.

Bonnie came to Andy and said, "who was that?"

"George Crossley, he offered to help Fred cook the cow on the spit, I said OK with me, but he had to ask Fred, and Fred was the boss."

"This is shapin up to be a humdinger of a shindig, now I'm getting excited, and in a little more than two months I'll be able to dance with you Andy dearest."

"wooo eeee, you and me, the purdiest lady, we'll be a makin the grass smoke with the stompin, the spinin and the jumpin we'll be doin.

"Andy, I can't wait to show off my new dress, I'm about ready to burst open with excitement. This shindig is going to be so much fun."

Andy said, "Can You give help to Janet with material to make a new dress, and I know Mark would appreciate this."

Meanwhile, when there were fifty-two days left before the stage coach came in, Art, Brownie, and William had arrived at Judge Roy Beans place.

The Judge said, "you boys made real good time riding down here. I received a telegram from my friend Andy. Andy said you boys spoke up for William and William would like to pay for the cows."

"Yes, sir, that's right."

"Andy wrote that you boys would be responsible for this owl hoot name of William Jones."

"Yes, sir, that's right, and if this man becomes unscrupulous and immoral and makes my boss and my friend Andy look bad, I'll be huntin him and bring him back to you either sitting up or lying across the horse, no matter to me which way."

Judge Roy Bean said, "William do you have anything to say before I give sentence."

"Your honor, Judge Roy Bean. I have seen the error of my ways, and I promise you, before the Almighty, that I will lead a straight life. I will turn away from the evil life that I had lived, and, I will also try to keep others from turnin to the evil way of life when I see them that want to do wrong."

"William, I want you to know I have never before in all my dealings in my court as the law in this area, never have I ever changed my mind, when I find them guilty, they stay guilty, and I send them to meet their maker." Judge Roy Bean unsheathed his gun from his shell belt holster. He banged the but on the saloon post and said, "William Jones of Wyoming, after careful deliberation, I declare you to be guilty of cattle rustling. This court directs you to remain in the custody of Andy Moonly on the Four Diamond Ranch. If ever I hear of you doing the shady sinful acts of cattle rustling again, I will issue an order to hang you on sight. If you ever leave the company of the Four Diamond Ranch, I will issue an order to hang you on sight. You sir, with the moniker of William Jones of Wyoming, are to be in custody and care of the Four Diamond Ranch. Andy Moonly has spoken up for you.

If you ever turn back to your wicked ways, I will come lookin for you myself. You are free to go on the provision that you remain in the custody of these two men Art and Brownie until you get to the Moonly Ranch. Then Andy is responsible for you, and if you take off from their charge or Andy's charge, then you are to be hunted down and killed on sight." Then Judge Roy Bean said, "William, Do you understand what this court has directed?"

"Yes sir Judge, I shorley do understand.I will be so respectable you won't ever hear of me or my name again."

"William Jones, I set store in Andy Moonly, and only Andy Moonly could have gotten you off, I will be askin my friend Andy Moonly about you periodically." Judge Roy Bean banged the butt handle of his gun on the veranda post and said: "This court is closed."

Art said, "Thank you, Judge, now if you will excuse us, we have to make tracks, Andy said we could not dally or be tardy, we must start back to the Four Diamond Ranch immediately."

"Art, when you get back to the ranch and see Andy, please give him my warmest regards, and please say a big howdy to Ken McKlay, these men were the best sheriff's I ever had workin for me."

"I shorley will Judge, goodbye for now and I'll give the message to Andy and Ken."

All three mounted their horses and started back, heading back to the Four Diamond Ranch near Monark.

Brownie said, "Let's make tracks and ride like the wind, we need to make between 70 and 100 miles every day, I have a big hankering to see the package come into Monark."

As they were riding along William Said, "Art, Brownie, I'll never forget what you have done for me. I was close to goin to see my maker, and at the last moment when the Judge said I'm in your care, I almost broke down, almost cried like a baby, I have never been that close to death before and then given a new chance. Boys, I promise you right here, right now, I will make you proud of me every day you see me, and I will do my best to earn your respect. I cannot say long enough or loud enough, thank you from the bottom of my heart."

Art said, "William, you know what the best thank you that we can ever have is, you have and keep high values. You go straight; you will always try your hardest to be there when we in the Moonly Fold have a problem. You will always be there as a guiding hand for others to see and as a guide for others to follow when every day you make Andy and Mark look good. Always remember, them that pays you money for a wage is the one to be protected, you work for the brand."

Thirty-six days later and still on the trail, Art said: "Look, way off in the distance, I can see Monark."

William said, "I'm getting excited, I can't wait to see Andy and give him a thank you. Also, I will promise him that I'll always do my best to be part of the ranch and not be a loner. I promise to ride for the brand."

Brownie said, "Art will you listen to this, I think this saddle pounder is already starting to get it and become part of the group, I think he's already on the mend."

Art said, "By jigger, just maybe your think bucket is bigger than a gopher's think bucket after all. I think he will become one of us faster than we thought."

William said, "Now I know you guys are funnin me, and that's alright, I've never felt like I was part of something before, and I never had people so close to me that I could say they are good friends, I am starting to like this."

Art said, "William, I'm beginning to think you'll be alright. Always remember to put your best foot forward so other people can see you for who you are. Always do the best you can, always protect your pard and always protect the brand you ride for, make it look good, make it look like you mean it with honesty and heart."

As time went on and many miles behind them and the days had passed Brownie said: "look, in about two hours we'll be able to see the Moonly Ranch in the distance, wooo eee, we'll be able to see the package come in, after all, we'll be able to see the package when it comes in on the stage. I'm lookin to see Norm's face when the package arrives; this otta be good."

Art said, "Boys if it's true about what they say about the package comin into Monark, this is going to be an exciting day for all of us."

William said, "Art, Brownie, what are you two talkin about; I don't know anything about any of this."

Art and Brownie smiled and looked at each other, and they both gave a wink.

Brownie said, "William my young lad, you have to wait and see, we can't tell you what's about to happen, just be patient and follow along young feller."

When they arrived at the Moonly Ranch, Andy saw them ride into the yard, he welcomed them back home and said: "let's all go to the house and have a coffee, and we'll have a talk."

13

When they walked into the kitchen, Andy said, "Bonnie, can you make the four of us a cup of coffee. We'll be in the parlor room sitting at the table having a confab."

Art said, "What would you like boss?"

"William, I have a job for you. I want a pit dug out on the right side of the house, about twenty-five feet from the house. The pit is to be four feet wide by eight feet long and two feet deep, then I need poplar, willow, and oak trees cut and put in the pit, I also need coal hauled over to the pit and put the coal on top of the wood for burnin."

Art said, "Boss, is it OK if we help William, I'm a thinkin he's startin to be a pard, and we'll help him in his start of the straight and narrow."

"Good idea, you and Brownie can help William, and after the pit is filled with wood and coal, I need a spit hung over the fire built so a body can turn the spit with something cookin on the spit and this needs to be strong enough to hold a whole cow. All this has to be built before the twenty-first of August, and you men have 20 days to complete this job, no if's and's or but's, this need to be done long before 21 August."

Bonnie brought the coffee for the four of them and said, "Here you are, would you like a piece of pie with this?"

"No thanks, Bonnie," Andy said.

Brownie said, "Boss, we'll have this built for you as fast as we can."

Then Andy passed on to the three about the party comin up, and about Ken and Lily, they are getting hitched on the 22nd August, and Norm and the package getting hitched on the 22nd also and the package is arriving on the 21 August. Andy also passed on the names of everyone that will be attending including the parson."

William asked, "Mister Moonly, can you tell me about this package that is arriving for the Sheriff?"

Andy saw Art and Brownie wink and shake their head from left to right in a no gesture.

Andy said, "William, you are just goin to have to wait and see."

"I am about to bust wide open; I'm so curious about what the package is, for the Sheriff."

Brownie said, "William, you just have to be patient like the rest of us."

Coffee done, Art said, "OK lads, let's go get the job done. William, you dig the hole, Brownie and I will get the wood. When we have the wood picked up and brought back, we can help you with the hole. Then the three of us can build a spit heavy enough to cook a cow."

All three started off to do their assigned work.

Andy rode into Monark to send a telegraph to the

Judge Roy Bean. When Andy arrived at the telegraph office, he wrote out the note "Judge Roy Bean STOP three men arrived STOP had a meeting and gave job STOP the first day is impressive STOP your friend Andy."

Andy said I'll come back later for the reply, and I know there will be one."

The telegraph operator sent off the note with the short and the long dots and the dashes clicking and clacking away as he worked.

In a few minutes after he sent the telegram, sure enough, the keys started clickin and clankin away again with the dots and dashes, the operator deciphered the code and wrote the reply down for Andy.

When Andy came back, the operator gave Andy the return note; Andy read the note which said "Glad to hear all is good STOP say hi to the best part of you STOP give my best to her STOP your friend Judge Roy Bean." Andy put the message in his pocket and walked out of the telegraph office.

Andy mounted up and rode back to the Moonly Ranch. As Andy was comin into the main yard site, Andy looked around and thought "yes, we have been lucky, lucky in cow sales, lucky in horse flesh, lucky in acres owned, lucky in business matters, and best of all was the addition of that new girl Lily to the Moonly roster. She sure is a crackerjack in the legal and finance matters, and she is a big help in guiding the Moonly Ranch forward, with her help the Moonly Ranch will be bigger and better than ever before, yes things were lookin up for sure."

When he reached the ranch house and walked inside to the kitchen area, he said loudly; "Bonnie where are you?"

"I'm here in the parlor area."

Andy walked into the parlor and said, "Bonnie, let's go to Monark and go see the sheriff and talk about the package, make sure everything is ready for the twenty-second."

Bonnie agreed and off they went.

Mark Moonly came walking towards the house and noticed the three men working on the pit and area.

Art said, "Before you ask, Andy gave us a job to do and have this done on or before the twenty-first of August, and he gave us fourteen days to do this, and we will be done very early."

"I just had a look, everything is OK, and I know about the jobs given for this here cookin pit, and I wanted to pass on that Andy and Bonnie have gone to Monark."

"OK, thanks, boss," Art said.

William said, "Boss, what is the package that has come in for the sheriff?"

Art and Brownie winked at Mark, then wagged their head left to right.

Mark said, "You will have to wait and see just like the rest of us, we'll all see the package on the twenty-first, and then the sheriff will bring the package out here on the twenty-second."

Brownie said, "Oooooeeeee, this is shore to be the biggest shindig, I've ever been to or seen!"

William said, "You boys are a makin me close to bust wide open with excitement, I can hardly wait!"

The saddle pounders came in from riding the range. One of the ranch hands, Jerry was his name, Jerry said,

"Mister Moonly all cows are counted for today, the numbers tally."

"Thanks, Jerry, please pass on to the other cow nurses, job well done! Don't forget the twenty-second of August, everyone here has the day off, and everyone is invited to the shindig, I expect everyone to have a bath and get cleaned up for this, please wear your Sunday go to meetin clothes."

Jerry hoofed it back quickly to the other ranch hands sleeping area and reiterated what Mark had said. All the ranch hands were talking with excitement, as this was the biggest thing to happen on the Moonly ranch, and even bigger than the time the new church was first used on Sunday.

Seven days have gone by, and in the morning for breakfast, the cook had bacon, flapjacks, and eggs for those that wanted eggs.

All the hands came in for breakfast. Andy and Bonnie came down to have breakfast with all the ranch hands.

As they were taking their seat for breakfast Andy said "Alright all you saddle pounders, let me have your attention. Bonnie and I went to Monark the other day. We have seen the sheriff and talked about the package comin on the stage on the 21 August.

Bonnie said "OK, my turn, the twenty-second is now comin closer, there are a few things we got to clear up. At this shindig, there are some rules that must be followed. One/ No fighting allowed atoll. Two/ No pushing allowed. Three/ No makin fun of somebody. Four/ No nasty remarks allowed. Five/ No makin anyone look bad. Six/ Have as much fun as you can within those guidelines.

Seven/ If any one of these rules is broken, then you will report to me, and gentlemen, let me assure you, Andy is a gentle pussy cat compared to what I will make you do If you ruin my gala event. For your information, the McKlay and Slinger Ranches are being told the same rules. Both the McKlay and Slingers agree with me and what I will do, and, if any of the other Ranches hired hands break the rules, then they will also work for me."

As Andy and Bonnie were leaving one of the ranch hands by the name of Rick Band, with a sneer had asked another ranch hand close by "What can she do to us, she's a girl?"

The other ranch hand by the name of Brian Bishop said "I had heard her say if anybody breaks the rules, no matter which Ranch, you work for, if you break the rules then you work for her for a week, or you quit. She has some nasty jobs picked out like diggin three new biffies on each ranch just for starters."

"Jiggers, she has a malicious streak, I think I'll come out on my best Sunday go to meetin behavior dressed in my best Sunday go to meetin clothes."

All the ranch hands that were in the room having breakfast thought this would be the best idea ever came about on the Moonly Ranch.

Andy came back into the room after Bonnie had left the room. Andy said; "Gentlemen, please do not get my wife riled, she has a firecracker attitude if you do her wrong. Trust me; you do not want to do her wrong. The diggin of the biffies, this is done with water being poured into the hole while your diggin, you'll be black with dirt and soaking in mud, and you'll be diggin in bare feet. If you ever get finished the first hole, and you have a week of this diggin or you quit. The other Ranches are being told the same rules, so please plan to get along. And trust me there are other surprises comin up at this shindig, which I think you will be amazed and will like when you see them, and there will be lots to eat, some drinks for the men, some games, and dance all night until the wee hours of the mornin."

When Andy came out from talking with the ranch hands, Bonnie said "Andy my dearest, can you send someone to the McKlay and Slinger Ranches and invite the women folk to come here for a meeting with me. We can start at about, oh let's say ten o'clock, and I also need the Parson to come out for this meeting."

"I'm on it; I'll track down Jack Tainan to ride out to do that job for you, he'll be goin as soon as I find him."

Andy went on the hunt to find Jack, and found him in the corral, getting ready to start breaking a horse to ride. Andy said, "Jack, my wife Bonnie has a job for you, she needs to have a meetin with the McKlay and Slinger Ranch ladies. Please ride to the ranches inviting the ladies to come here for Ten O'clock. Then you need to ride to Monark and invite the Parson to come to this meetin as well. Oh, by the way, Jack, don't spare the horse flesh, make it as fast as you can."

"Will do boss, I'll saddle up the fastest horse I have and leave right away."

Andy left and went over to look at the fire pit being dug, and he saw William with his shirt off workin as fast as he could, and the dirt was flying over his shoulder. William also had perspiration running off his head and arms and running down his chest, back and dribbling down his muscled torso.

Andy said, "William, you don't have to work that hard, I don't want you to be killin yourself doin this."

"Yes, I do boss, I have done wrong, and now I'm payin for it, now I'm doin the best job I can the fastest I can so I can get on to another job. You stuck your neck way out for me; now I'm payin you back for all your help, faith and support you have given me."

"Tell you what I'll do, you keep workin this way when it comes time to pay for those cows you took, I'll help you pay for them."

"Boss, where were you when I was a youngster, I needed somebody like you to show me between right and wrong."

14

"William, I'll tell you the truth, I was lucky, my pa showed Mark and me how to be the best we can. Most days he was not gentle either, for example, if we came in late or I mean early in the mornin from a dance, he worked us harder that day, and we never had any sleep yet, he kept us honest, starting from the time we could remember. Dad gave us credit and said we did good when we worked hard, and he scolded us when we didn't. He also taught us that we are only as good as what we say. Then there is my mom; she taught us that it's OK to cry and cryin is part of growin and healin. She also taught us that if we swear or say the words nobody likes to hear, that makes us look like we do not know the English language or know how to speak good English. Trust me she could swat us same as dad did. When I remember back, I think she would swat us the hardest. When we were younguns, mom had even put lye soap in our mouth if we ever said a swear word. Both of them taught us to treat people like people and give them the benefit of the doubt. Let them prove they are worthy or not worthy to be on my side and most important they gave us strong, hard, honest values to live by."

"Boss, I shore want to show you that I can be on your side, and I shore do wish I could have met you earlier. I think I would have been different today had I met you earlier."

"William, you keep workin this way, and for every dollar that you pay, I will match it and give the money to you so you can pay for those cows fast."

"Boss I need to get diggin and make this pit ready soon as I can."

When Andy was walking towards the house, he saw a horse and buggy comin from the way of McKlay Ranch. It looks like the ladies are starting to come for the hen meeting already. Andy thought best I stay away from the house and stay out of reach of that hen party. There could be some laughing, cackling and much talkin going on today, in that kitchen.

Mark came up and said, "Big brother, in one month we should start brandin season again, do we have everything we need for this big round up?"

"Matter a fact we do, I picked up four brand new ropes the other day and even bought a new ropin saddle in case one breaks down with the horn and bridge torn off. We have new horseshoes and lots of nails for attachin those horseshoes. We have a wagon load of coal for Fred Morgan to keep the fire hot both in the blacksmith shed and out on the prairie. Mark, I am shore glad Fred is our smithy, Fred can fasten horseshoes on a horse, faster than anybody I ever saw. In branding, he can brand three cows to others doing one. Fred, yes he is extremely good at his job. Brandin time, yes we are definitely ready. Matter a fact; I saw Fred look after a deformed cow with one leg shorter than the other three. Well, Fred, he just walked up ever so calm like took a three- second look at the bottom hoof, then he went back and made a split shoe for the cow. I never saw this before, and it fit perfect, yes we are without a doubt ready."

"Alright, we can start planning for the first week of September to start brandin."

"Bonnie has invited Janet, the ladies from the McKlay and Slinger Ranches as well as the parson here. She wants to have a meetin before the twenty-second party comes about and we have a shindig. I know Bonnie wants to set up a list of all the festivities, she wants to have everything from marksmanship for the men, and a flour sack carry for the ladies and more. Then it will be the parson to stand up with Ken and Lily. Then it will be time for the sheriff to show the package what come in.

Then it's time to eat, after eating is done, we have the dance. With all the music and all the stompin and a rompin goin on we should be havin a pretty good time with people laughin, a talkin, and a dancin."

"Big brother, you, and Bonnie have done this up pretty good."

"Not me, Bonnie has done it all. She is the one that has come up with all the idea's to make this the best shindig we have had in a long time. In fact, we will even have a fiddle, a squeeze box, and a pie-anie here for the music. The Mayor will be up front a callin the dance, but before that starts, I'll take all the men that are ranch owners into the parlor, all the ranch hands will meet at the Coral area.

Then we all have a glass of my best whiskey. This whiskey is imported from a place called Quebec City."

"Andy, Bonnie, Janet and I are goin to dance together again, and I know Janet made a new dress just for this party. I'm getting excited about everybody comin here to have a good time."

Andy said, "Bonnie is going over to the McKlay Ranch today, to buy potatoes to cook and have beside the cow being cooked on the spit."

"This is goin to be the best and biggest gatherin this side of Boom Town, something for everyone here; this is going to be good. Big brother, the ladies from the ranches have arrived, and I see the parson's buggy is comin down the road."

"Don't go in the house little brother, the hen party will be a cackling soon; I don't know how the Parson can stay in there with all them women."

"Mark, I wanted to tell you, the other day I was in Monark. I went to see that new lady that's workin for us, she has already made a few recommendations, and she will be bringin them out here in about one week after the party. She is doing amazing work, shore glad you thought of offering her a job. I also stopped and seen that new feller William, he is goin ta be all right, he is one very hard worker, he might even set the bar as to how hard the men will have to work."

"We really don't want to upset that apple cart, let's try and keep the same standard for work as we were taught if we try to put in more we might have a squabble on our hands."

"Your right Mark, but he is one hard worker, he is not

a skeared to get his hands dirty, and he is not fearful of work atoll."

Bonnie welcomed the ladies and the parson into the Moonly Ranch house. When everyone was seated in the parlor, Bonnie said, "Ladies and Parson there are a few things we have to complete before the twenty-second. Annett and Joan McKlay, how is the wedding dress for Lily coming along. Parson how is the package for the sheriff coming along. Ladies of the McKlay Ranch I'll be going out to your ranch this afternoon to buy potatoes, carrots, and turnips to cook and have with the cow we will cook on the spit. Esther, Annett, and Joan can you three make buns for the people to eat, about two dozen buns each should do it. Does anybody else have anything to say?

Annett said, "Yes, I'll make two dozen buns. Lily's dress is all completed, and she sure looks good in that dress. Ken is going to Monark every day after work to see Lily, and, I must admit I like her too. She is not afraid of work, and she is not a lazy person, oh my, she is very active."

Esther said, "Yes, I'll make the buns and is there anything else you would like."

Joan said, "I'm on it, I'll make the buns you requested, is two dozen from each of us enough?"

"I think two dozen will be enough, that'll give us 72 buns, this should be enough."

The Parson said, "As a matter of a fact the package is on time, the package arrives before 2:30 in the afternoon of the 21 this month and I'm all set to marry the two couples."

"Anybody else have anything to say?" Bonnie asked

Annett asked, "Do you need help cooking the food on the spit and maybe help in cooking the potatoes?"

"No, OK then, Fred Benson is coming out to do the cooking. He has used the spit many times, and he even knows how to cook the potatoes beside the open fire and not burn them. I think he called it a baked potato. We have William, who will be helping Fred turn the spit while Fred puts on some of his special spices. Larry will do the basting, and George Crossley will help also. Anybody else have any questions?"

"Esther from the Slinger Ranch said, "what about a ruckus, what happens then?"

"That is not to worry, I have already seen the men folk of the Slinger Ranch, the McKlay Ranch, and the Moonly Ranch. If there is a ruckus, then after the party for a week the men who are in the ruckus work for me, for a week. They will not like what they will have to do. They'll be digging three outhouses on the ranch they come from, in the mud in their bare feet."

All the ladies giggle, and the parson looked at the floor.

Joan still giggling said, "Bonnie, you have single handily figured out how to control these bantam roosters, when they start a strutting around and taken a poke at someone."

Bonnie said "Ladies I forgot to mention, Judge Roy Bean is a friend of Andy's, and he will be here for this party, Andy does not know this yet, and I'm trying to keep this as a surprise to Andy. Andy keeps talking so much about the Judge, and the telegram I see from the Judge, he also likes Andy. I want to see Andy's eyes when the Judge shows up, so please don't mention this too much."

Annett said, "Don't forget Ken, he worked for Judge Roy Bean as a sheriff about six years ago."

The other ladies and the parson were all in a tight conversation, the gist of it was about keeping people interested in this event, then the Parson said: "There will be many people who will want to talk to the Judge and listen to some of his many stories."

Bonnie said, "Esther, I'm waiting to hear from Wild Bill Hitchcock, I understand Hubert was friends with him, I am waiting for a telegram from him to confirm if he can make it up here."

"You have been a busy girl doing all this, how do you find the time and how do you keep it quiet from everybody else?"

"Oh, I just mosey along, look like I am not interested in too much in Monark. When the boys are out of sight, or I go into town alone, then I can look after my affairs. I also ask the telegraph operator to keep things quiet as sometimes there could be gifts going on with people coming in here, and I am trying to have a surprise for people. Today, after the McKlay Ranch, I'll go to Monark for a few things at the mercantile, and I'll also stop off and see the telegraph operator, see if there is a message from Wild Bill."

"OK ladies and Parson, I think we have everything in hand and ready for the twenty-second."

Everybody stood up and started to walk to the door saying their good-bye's.

As the people were walking out the door, Bonnie

thanked them for coming out to discuss the twenty-second schedule and finalize all that is left for this gala event.

When everybody had driven away in their horse and buggy, Bonnie walked to where William was digging the pit. Just as she walked up to William, he had just finished digging the size of the pit that he was told to dig.

Bonnie said, "Hello William, I am amazed that you have the pit dug already, this looks exactly like what I had wanted, what I had asked for, and what is needed for cookin of the cow."

"You're mighty welcome misses."

"Where have the other two ranch hands got to."

"They have gone to bring back firewood, which can then be mixed with the coal for burnin in the pit. Now I'm off to make a cookin spit to be placed over the pit to cook a cow on"

"William, I am very happy with the work you are turning out, and I will pass this on to Andy and Mark, thank you so much for doing this excellent job for me."

"Thank you misses, now if you will excuse me, I have to go to the blacksmith shed to start makin a cookin spit for this here cookin-pit."

Art and Brownie were just coming into the pit area when William started to walk away.

William said, "Hi boys, pit's all dug, Andy's misses seen the pit and likes it, now I'm off to the blacksmith shop to start makin the spit."

Art said, "Soon as we're done here, we'll come help you make the spit and then we'll bring it over here and set it up over the pit."

After the coal and wood had been put into the fire pit, Art and Brownie helped William, in two hours the cooking spit was finished. They hand carried the spit over to the pit and positioned the spit over the cooking pit. The three men shared the work of digging the holes to put the cooking spit legs into and hold the spit tight. When everything was built and installed in the pit, the boys looked at their finished job, and they all agreed it was a piece of work to be proud of, this spit looked better than great!

15

E very day, after work on the ranch looking after the chicken house and garden areas, Ken would wash up, get dressed in his Sunday go to meetin clothes, then ride into town to see Lily.

On one of those days Lily asked, "Ken, can you tell me how the ranch you're on became known as the Broken Spur Ranch?"

"Well, that's an easy one, we had rounded up some Mustangs, and one of them was a strong willed palomino stallion. Well, I up and jumped on this horse, to break for riding. Well, you never saw a show like we put on that day. I was up and down, I was a side to side, I was near the front withers than the back haunches, and all the while this Mustang is trying to kick the spots off the moon. Well, like I was a saying, we were up and down, side to side and a twisting to and fro, then he tried to stand up on his two back legs. Well over we went, and at one point I was on the bottom, and he was on top, but I was still in the saddle. Well, I got out of that mess, then I got back in the saddle again, before he could run off. Well, he was up and down again, then he jumped the corral fence with me still in the saddle, and off we went faster than a dog chasing a bone. Well, I rode him a running as fast as he wanted to run. I wore him out, and when I finally came back to the ranch, his head was hanging down to his front feet. He was plum wore out with his tongue hanging out and his breathing harder than a forge fan blowing air. Today he's the best horse we have on the ranch. Well, when we came back to the ranch, and I climbed off that bronc, I looked down, only half my spur was left on the right foot. From that day to this, the ranch is known as the One Broken Spur Ranch.

"Ken is that true or are you just making fun of me?"

"Oh no, I'm not making fun of you, that is really how this ranch got to be known as the One Broken Spur Ranch, and our brand is also a Broken Spur, you can even ask my brothers Jim and Bob."

"Now what do you say we go to Fred's place for a meal, I'll buy you a meal and show off the best girl in Monark."

When they walked into Fred's place, there was only one table left; Ken held the chair for Lily until she was seated, and he pushed the chair in towards the table for Lily. Most of the people sat and looked slack jawed because they had never seen this side of Ken McKlay. Sure he and his brothers were always dressed up and looked good in their Sunday go to meeting clothes when they came to town, but they never showed this cultured and gentle side, they were always rough, tough and steely-eyed.

Ken took his seat across from Lily and said, "The twenty-second is coming up soon, the Moonly Brothers are giving us a wedding present of having the wedding at their ranch. They are also having a cow cooked on a spit with Fred cooking. We are also getting enough wood and

Portland cement from the Stuart Warress Lumber Yard, to make a house just for us, if we want to build a house."

"Ken, please tell me why they are doing all this for us?"

"Years back, we did not have very much, we all had to work hard, and we all worked pretty close together to make everything we needed. We still do when there is a need, but it seems when the children come along, families have their own things to do and plan for in their respective families. The closeness slowly wanes, and we slowly drift apart from the closeness we experienced before.

Well, at one point I had found a large herd of cows, some of them were mired in the mud. I pulled all the cows out with my horse and rope; then I showed Andy and Mark the mud hole so they could keep the cows away from there. From that point on, they've had a soft part for me."

"Are you always this gallant with everyone?"

"Lily, you know more than anyone else, I am who I am. I have my strong convictions that were passed on to me by my Ma and Pa, and I live by them. I don't lie; I don't cheat, I don't steal, I don't make anyone look bad, I don't embarrass anyone on purpose, I don't take credit for someone else's work. I stand up for those that can't stand up for themselves, and everything else is fair game, just like the day I saw that man Jim do you wrong when he reached across and gave you a swat."

Fred's helper, the waiter, named Berry Salvas came over and said: "Today for supper we have Spareribs, Potatoes, and Parsnips with Apple Pie for dessert, is this OK?"

Ken said, "Yes that will be fine, may we each have a plate of this. Can you also bring us two coffee's?"

"Right away Mister McKlay, good to see you again."

"Please say a big howdy to that old buffalo hunter in the back; I still think the sun rises on him every day, I have a lot a time for Fred."

Lily asked, "Why do you like Fred so much?"

"That's easy when we were building the main house on the Broken Spur Ranch, Fred came out to the ranch every day to help us build that log cabin we live in now. Fred worked harder than any man I had ever seen work. Fred worked for seven days in the bush cutting down trees, then he carried the trees to the logging skidder, when he brought the trees up to the house area, he even notched the trees to be put them in place to make the house. Fred and I have been good friends ever since, and if he ever said he needed help, I would instantly drop what I was doing, then I would run to be the first one where he is, as fast as I could, so that I could help him do what was needed."

"Does everybody in this area work that closely together to build houses and barns?"

"As a matter a fact, yes they do. When people first came to this area, there weren't too much to be had. Whatever we could get we had to build, and the people helped one another to have or make these things. Heck, we never even locked the house door, we never had to, people respected other people, and what the other person had. Everybody had to work hard to get what they wanted; everybody was taught if it isn't yours don't touch it."

Larry brought the meal out to Ken and Lily and placed it down on the table in front of them, and then Larry said; "I'll bring the coffee right away folks."

Fred came over and placed a chair beside the table and sat down.

Ken said, "Fred you old buffalo herdsman, how are you doing this evening."

Fred in his low, hoarse and coarse voice said: "If I were any better, you and I would be brothers, and we would be out on the town, just howling at the moon."

"Sorry Fred, I can't do that anymore, I've thrown my rope around this here little filly, and on the twenty-second this little filly, Lily is her name, she and I are going to be hitched. This is going to be the best day of my life, yahoooo! Fred meet Lily; Lily meet my friend Fred."

"I hear ya, and I know what ya mean, the best part of me is back home, her name is Christie, she is one of a kind, and she is the best that has ever happened to me. Nice to meet you, Lily."

Lily said, "Nice to meet you, Fred."

Ken said, "Fred my friend, are you going to bring Christie out to the Moonly Ranch on the twenty-second of this month, I for one would sure like to see you and your family there."

"Now Ken, I daren't go anywhere without Christie, she would set me straight first thing, and then I'd feel bad because I would have done her wrong, oh yes she'll be there all right, you can count on it."

Back at the Moonly Ranch, Bonnie had the horse and buckboard hitched up and drove to the McKlay Ranch; she picked up ten chickens, fifty pounds of potatoes, ten pounds of carrots and 6 pounds of parsnips. She brought these items back to the four diamonds Ranch and unloaded the wagon; she put the chickens in the hen house, then she took the horse and wagon to the barn and asked Jack Tainan if he would unhitch the horse from the wagon and hitch the horse up to the buggy.

"Shore will, ma'am right away."

When the horse was hitched up to the buggy, Bonnie climbed on up into the buggy and headed towards Monark; she needed to see the telegraph operator and check on Andy's gift. The afternoon ride to Monark was so peaceful; the day was warm and sunny, Bonnie felt warm all over, and she thought about herself and her man. The birds were chirpin in the trees, once in a while, a rabbit would bound away from the path leading to Monark. Overhead a hawk was lazily circling, looking for food. She noticed that the hawk had swooped down, picked up a rabbit and flew away to where ever the nest was. Bonnie thought sometimes this old world could be tough, dog eat dog world, the big dog eats the little dog, and somewhere there is always a bigger dog just waiting. Bonnie thought how lucky she was that she met Andy. Together with Mark and Janet they planned and worked, then worked and planned, and now things were starting to shape up and come together. The hard work was starting to show fruit for the hard toil of labor they had done. She remembered some days past when they lived in the sod house; she would feel so sore when she went to bed. Bonnie felt just plumb worn out from the days of hard work she was doing, working beside Andy to make this a workable and profitable ranch. She remembered all this and was thankful that things were now coming together.

When she arrived at the Telegraph office, she went

inside and said: "Good afternoon Bernie, anything come in for me?"

"As a matter a fact, ma'am, yes, there is a telegram for you, say's it's from the judge."

Bonnie's felt like her heart skip a beat and then started to beat faster. She couldn't rip the envelope open fast enough. Finally, she had the paper out and read the telegram, "Good day Bonnie, so good to hear from you STOP. My wife and I have already started the trip a couple of weeks ago STOP. I am glad you and Andy are doing well STOP. Thank you for the invite to this planned and grand event STOP. Yes, I will try my best to be there for this event STOP. Yes, I will bring my misses STOP. I think Andy's eyes will bulge out when he see's us STOP. See you on the twenty-first STOP. Your friend the judge."

Bonnie smiled the biggest smile she had had in a long time; then she put the telegram in her handbag and walked over to the boarding house.

The boarding house was owned and operated by a woman with the name Sherry, no one knew where she came from or what she did before coming here, but she seemed like a friendly, honest, hard working and a good person.

When she arrived at the boarding house, she said; "Good afternoon Sherry, a friend of Andy's and mine, he and his wife are coming to town, please put them up in the best room you have and give me the bill, you are not to take money from my guest. Andy is not to know about this, as this is a surprise, and Andy has not seen him in quite a few years. The guest's name is Judge Roy Bean."

Sherry looked up with a start and said, "Yes Bonnie

I will do that for you, now tell me how did you meet this man?"

"When you come out to the ranch on the twenty-second, I'm sure that will come up in the conversation, see you later, and thank you."

Bonnie went over to Fred's place; she wanted to check with Fred to make sure all is set and ready.

Fred said in his low, hoarse and coarse voice, "You bet, I'll be out at your place on the twenty-first and start cookin at one o'clock in the morning. The cow will take a while to cook, do you think Andy can give me a little of his special stock? I'll use this to make a base; this is required to brush on the cow when cookin on the spit.

"I'll pass the request on to Andy for you, and thank you again for doing this for us."

"My pleasure Bonnie."

Bonnie had completed her business in town and started driving the horse and buggy home. She thought things were coming together for this shindig, and Andy was going to be surprised. When the Judge and his wife come to town, I need to hide them away and have him come out just at the right moment. I think maybe when Andy is in the shooting competition, then this would be the right moment for the Judge to come forward.

As she was going home, coming toward her on his horse was Jim McKlay. She heard Jim yodeling, and the sound was downright pleasurable. She remembered that whenever he was on his horse, he always seemed more calm and relaxed. He was always yodeling when he was riding the horse, and really, the yodeling she had to admit did sound pretty good, and she thought the horse liked it too because one the horse's ears were always turned backward to listen. Bonnie thought, sometimes Jim would yodel "O DEE O, DI DA, YAY YODEL O HO DEE." Sometimes he would yodel the cattle song, "OOO DOO OOOO, UU DEE, OOO DOO OOO DOOP DA DOO, DOO DOO OOO DOO OOOO, UU DEE O DA LOW A UH OOOO DEE, THIS IS THE CATTLE SONG."

"Afternoon Jim, how is your day, everything good at home I trust."

"Afternoon Bonnie, yes, things are top notch, say a big howdy to Andy."

"And you to Annett, good day to you, see you both on the Moonly Ranch on the twenty-second."

"We'll be there."

After Jim had passed, Bonnie thought this was a good neighbor, always willing to help out when required or asked; he was without a doubt the salt of the earth. She wondered why more people couldn't be like him and maybe some people in and around Monark. People that work at getting along, the ones that work hard, do not gossip, and the ones who do not tear down someone else's work.

16

B onnie looked up in awe when she was driving the horse and buggy home; she saw an eagle soaring ever so gracefully, gliding back and forth across the sky looking for its dinner. She thought she knew now what it meant when somebody said eye of an eagle. To be that high up, soaring along and see a tiny mouse running from tree to tree. To think an eagle, from that high up can see this little guy, and to see him running, this is one of the wonders that we have in this world. As she was going along driving the buggy, a rabbit jumped out of the bush just behind the horse and in front of the wagon. The horse spooked and took off with a lurch and a jump; the buggy started to bounce. Bonnie's hat came down over one eye, she had hold of the reins tight, but could not move her hand to straighten her hat. She thought, "I'll never wear a hat again when I'm driving a horse and buggy or wagon; I can always put it on when I stop the buggy." To make matters worse, the horse was still picking up speed, and she couldn't seem to slow the horse down. All of a sudden the horse took a sharp left, the buggy tilted up on two wheels, then it seemed to bounce up, bang down and then right itself. She felt it slam down on the four wheels again. Bonnie felt the wind in her cheeks and lower face, the horse seemed to be going faster. She pulled back on the reins and still nothing happened, by this time the buggy was bouncing and careening, and, it seems like the buggy was bouncing from the two left side wheels to the two right side wheels. Bonnie braced her feet on the front of the buggy and pulled back with all her strength; she was pulling so hard her arms were starting to vibrate violently. She thought, "OH I'll never see Andy again. I'll never get to laugh and joke with him again; I never feel him tickle me. If I ever get out of this, I'll never get mad at him again, especially when he tickles me. Then she thought of how much she loved Andy and how much he meant to her. She remembered the low, soft tones in his voice when he said I love you. She pulled back a little harder. What's this, it feels like the buggy is slowing down. She pulled on the reins so hard she thought she would break them, and it felt like her arms were vibrating with the strain. All of a sudden out of nowhere along came Ken McKlay. Looking with only one eye not covered by her hat, it looked like everything was in very slow motion, while she was being bounced along in the front seat. She looked in fascination while holding on and it seemed Ken just rode up ever so slowly, he slowly, gracefully and steadily reached down and grabbed hold of the bridle, and then he ever so gently slowed the horse down. He made it look so easy and yet she knew she was going faster than she had ever gone before in all her life. When the buggy finally stopped, she was still so frightened she couldn't say or even mumble any words. There seemed to be a lump swelling up inside her throat making it hard to swallow; there were also big tears forming in her eyes and streaming down her face. After what seemed like many minutes, she reached up and removed her hat.

Finally, she said "Ken, thank heavens, you were here, a rabbit scared my horse, and I couldn't stop him. I pulled and pulled on the reins, and nothing seemed to work. Thank you so much, I can never repay you for what you've done for me. How do I begin to pay you for this, you have, I think saved my life."

"Bonnie, don't you fret none. I just happened to be out this way and see you had a bit of trouble."

"Ken, about one to two weeks after you two are married, you bring that wife of yours out to the ranch, you two stay the night, and I'll make you the biggest and best-tasting steak dinner you have ever eaten."

"Done, paid in full, we'll be there."

Bonnie got out of the buggy and said: "I think I'll walk home."

"Ask Andy to put a set of blinders on the bridle; this will stop the horse being spooked from the sights and shadows behind."

As Bonnie started to walk away leading the horse she said: "Thanks ever so much Ken, see you on the twenty-second."

Bonnie was walking and thinking of the peril she was in, and she started to shake. She started to feel cold, which made her shake even more. I wonder she thought, "Is there anything to them that think there is a Guardian Angel or some power looking out for you?"

When she finally got home her legs were so tired, they

felt like a buzzing going on in the lower legs, and her feet were sore, never had her feet felt this sore. When she saw Andy, she folded herself into his arms, molding herself to Andy, and sobbed, the big teardrops sliding down from her eyes and falling from her face to the floor. The very big sobs that sounded like they were coming all the way from her feet. Bonnie thought, "I feel so safe and secure all wrapped up in Andy's powerful arms." Bonnie explained to Andy about everything that happened to her on the way home; then she said, "Andy, I promise I will never get mad at you ever again. You are my life. You are the center of my life. I realized that you make my life so much more than what it was before I met and married you. You complete my life, and I will never raise my voice to you again, I will never get mad at you again, never-never-never, I promise. You big lug, I love you more and more every day!"

Andy held her like he had never held her before and said "you have just said everything I feel for you, and without you, my life is nothing, my life is not bright or white it is black and dismal. You make my life complete, and you make our life happy. You make our house warm and inviting. Without you, I feel helpless and lost. He gave her a kiss that was so strong Bonnie knees seemed to buckle, and she became breathless.

Panting Bonnie said, "Now that's love."

After Supper, Andy and Bonnie went for a walk to see how the different projects were coming along.

Andy said "That new man, William, in just a few days he has done more than most men have done in a week here on the ranch, and he looks for more. Look at this cookin spit, top drawer, couldn't be better even if I had done this myself."

Bonnie agreed and said "Tomorrow is the twenty-first, the stage comes to town tomorrow, and we'll have to go to town early. Fred will be out here tonight, at the crack o dark, he'll start the fire, at about one in the morning he'll start to cook the cow on the cookin spit, and it will still be so dark outside."

"Yes, we'll start out for the town right after breakfast."

"Andy my darling, after Ken had stopped the horse and buggy for me, possibly saving my life, he suggested that you put blinders on the driving bridle, he had said this would stop the horse from being spooked from behind in a blind spot."

"I'll do better than that; I will also put a new bridle together, I'm thinking a spade bit to stop the steel or harsh mouth of the horse and then the horse will respond better to stopping, as well as putting the blinders on the bridle."

"Thank you, Andy, you have always been there for me, and you have always given me support when I need it."

"Listen, babe you are not only my best friend, but you are also the light in my life. Without you, my life would be dark and dull with very little light, I am yours, and I belong to you, I love only you with all my heart, and I want to be beside you for the rest of my life."

"Andy change of subject, everything looks ready here, tomorrow is going to be a splendid day with the arrival of the package, and the twenty-second is going to be a fabulous day when the package arrives here. The Parson is ready and has everything in hand, and oh, by the way,

I have a surprise gift for you that should be ready for the twenty-second, don't ask, it's a surprise."

"Bonnie," Andy said, "I know you, and how that marvelous mind of yours works, this could be anything."

"Don't ask, it's a surprise, and I have the time of my life, and my jollies keeping you in suspense."

"You are sadistic when you want to be."

Bonnie said, "Let's go in before it gets too dark to see."

"Alright," Andy led the way holding Bonnie's hand.

When morning arrived, they were up bright and early, ready to have breakfast at 6:00 o'clock. After breakfast, Andy went out and hooked up the horse and buggy. The buggy was big enough to seat the four people, Mark, Janet, Bonnie, and Andy for the trip to Monark to watch the stage coach come into town.

After the horse and buggy had been hitched up together and ready to go, Andy walked towards the house and passed on the information that the horse and buggy were all ready for the trip into Monark.

Janet said, "I have this new hat that I can wear for the trip to town, the hat came all the way from Boom Town."

Mark said, "Sweetheart, you look good in anything you wear."

Bonnie said, "I'll only wear a hat in the buggy when I'm not driving, last time taught me a great lesson, I need both of my eyes for driving the horse and buggy."

Janet said, "In case I forget, we need to put a coffee pot and cups outside for Fred while he is here cooking."

Mark said, "I'm on it."

Bonnie said, "Andy, Fred asked if he could have some of your special stock to make a base for basting the cow?"

"I'll have it put beside the pit for Fred."

At ten o'clock everybody piled into the buggy and Andy started the horse with a "Giddyup Blacky." Away they went with a laughing and singing; they started the singsong with Camp Town Ladies. After the singing died down Mark said: "Remember on Tuesday, 21 August, the stagecoach arrives in Monark at 2:25 PM."

When they arrived in town, there is already an enormous amount of people who had come to town, waiting to see the stage coach with all its passengers come racing into town and then grinding to a halt.

Andy heard the stage coming before he could see the cloud of dust at the south end of town. Then he heard the rumble of the steel rim covered wood wheels and the galloping of the six-horse team. The six chargers are pulling the stagecoach up the road toward Monark, and still in the distance; he heard the clear, crisp voice of Larry, the driver, GIDDYUP THERE HAAAH!, then the loud, crisp crack of the whip sound. Andy pulled his watch out of his pocket and looked at it, the time read 2:20 in the afternoon and the stage is right on time. As the stagecoach was coming closer to the hotel, Andy heard Larry yell loudly, "WHOA YOU BUNCH OF NAGS WHOA!" When the stagecoach driver stopped the stagecoach, it was right across from the Monark Hotel; Andy thought pretty good driving. Andy remembered Larry grew up in Monark, he and Larry use to play together when they were kids. Strange how life takes us away from things we grow up with when we are kids. Larry and I only say hello now when we meet on the street.

The Stage driver after putting the wheel brake

on climbed to the top roof storage area and started to hand the carpet bags and the trunks down. The stage door opened and stepping down from the stage ever so daintily is a young lady that this side of the world has never seen before. This young lady, according to the Mail Order Bride section in the catalog, on page thirty-five, is a young woman, 27 years old and speaks good English. This young lady even though she is older than she looks, she looks to be about 15 Years old. The stage driver yells very loudly "Alooncee Gornphun, here are your carpet bags and trunks."

Aroonsri said in perfect English, "Mr. Stage Coach Driver, thank you for a perfect trip, and your help with my carpet bags and my trunks." Aroonsri Gornphun, dressed in what looked to be the brightest, reddest, longest, shirt with trousers to match. This shirt and trousers, made from a shining material which seemed very light in weight. On the shirt and trousers are many white flying dragons and there is a white string belt around her waist to show her slim hourglass figure. She has white colored socks and low cut shoes with very low heels. Her hair is black as coal and is all tied up in a big round bun with a stick hairpin that holds the hair together, and yet the hair ends seem to stick straight up from the back of her head, and when her hair is let down, it reaches the small of her back. Aroonsri's cheeks are rosy red, and her eyes are the biggest, deepest, darkest brown, you have ever seen. These eyes look so deep brown, they are almost black the same color as her hair, and her eyes glitter and gleam like there are many thousand diamonds in her eyes that make them glisten, gleam, and shine. Her lips are very bright red and well formed with the bottom a full pouty lip. When this fair maiden walks, it looks like she glides on air, while her back is straight as a poker.

The Mayor said to Norm, "This young lady is absolutely the prettiest gal that has ever come to Monark, and that is for shore. If her sisters and others look anything like Aroonsri Gornphun, there may be quite a few more Mail Order Brides comin to Monark."

Norm said, "This town has never seen so many people come to see the stage coach arrive in Monark, I am plumb impressed at the number of people come to town. Look there are all the McKlay boys with wives and Ken with his girlfriend, the Moonly Brothers, and Wives, practically the whole town came out to see."

"Norm, that lady coming to Monark is the biggest news we've ever had in this town, even bigger than when we heard William Bonnie was comin this way."

17

Norm quickly walked up to Aroonsri and said: "Miss Gornphun, my name in Norman John, I sent for you to come to Monark, and I have been practicing, saw wah dee mai krupt sow noi."

"Sa bai dee, thank you, you said, are you good and I answered I am good. You are doing well in learning to speak the language from Siam. I do not want to offend anyone, but sometimes my English is no good, I'm learning to speak English, the R's sound like L's and the L's sounds like R's."

"Miss Gornphun, I will have somebody bring your trunks and carpet bags to my house, er, I mean, our house and in the house, you will have your own room."

"Norman, please call me Aroonsri."

"Aroonsri, tomorrow, we have a shindig to go to, my friend Andy Moonly and his wife will have put on a cow roast, and a night of dancing, in honor of you comin to Monark, and we will also be married there."

"I am going to be busy, learning new things here and I am going to enjoy meeting all your friends and living in this little town, where I come from, the town looks to be about the same size but I think maybe two or three times the number of people of people here."

As Aroonsri and Norm reached their house, Bob Little with the livery-barn wagon was just leaving, and Aroonsri's trunks and carpet bags were up by the front door.

"Norm, you do have nice people here in this town, are everyone always ready to help like this?"

"You know it, everybody here in town and on the ranches, they all know you were comin in on the stage today, and they kept asking me when are you comin in?"

Aroonsri said, "Everybody is trying so hard to make me feel welcome."

Annett came walking up to the front door and said "Norm, you have to go for a walk, this lady and I have things we have to do now and you can't see or watch, go for a whiskey at the saloon.

When Norm left, Annett said "Miss Gornphun, we have to work fast, tomorrow there is the wedding for you and Norm and afterward a roasted cow on a spit, potatoes, and vegetables, dinner, and dance. I am here to make sure you have a wedding dress for tomorrow."

"Thank you for looking after me and making sure everything is in order, yes, I do have a wedding dress, and it is the traditional wedding dress that the people from Siam wear when they get married."

"May I see this dress you have?"

Aroonsri dragged one of her trunks over, unlocked the trunk and opened the lid; then she lifted out very many different colored clothing. Finally, she gently lifted out a warm pink colored dress with some white elephants on the dress, from the trunk; she lifted the dress high into the air.

Aroonsri said, "Here is my wedding dress, what do you think of this?"

Annett felt the cloth and said, "This is the finest and best silk I have ever seen, I can't buy anything like this here or anywhere around here, you are going to be the talk of the town when you are getting married, OK let's go find Norm."

Aroonsri gently packed the wedding dress and all the other clothing back in the trunk again.

Annett and Aroonsri walked arm in arm back to where Annett thought Norm would be. Just then the Parson walked close to them.

Annett said to the Parson, "Parson, this is Aroonsri, she is Norm's wife to be, and I must say, Parson, I have seen the finest silk that has ever come to Monark. I have never seen silk made this nice, not in all my life. No, sir, I have never seen this kind of silk, and, the sheriff is like a little kid when he gets close to this young lady, you should see how his chest pops out."

"Glad to hear that, I have coffee with the sheriff every once in a while and he does look like he is walking on air."

Annett said, "Here's Norm now," and as Norm walked up, Annett said, "Norm, here is your new bride to be; she is a very nice young lady, very polite."

Aroonsri put her hands together as if she were going to worship; then she said: "Hello Norm, I will do all I can to help you, be with you always and always try to have Nam Jai."

"What do you say we go to Fred's place and get you something to eat?"

"How did you know I was feeling hungry, the bouncing in that wooden box made me hungry?"

Norm laughed and said "yes, we do have some things to learn, but it's OK. Aroonsri what does Nam Jai mean?"

Aroonsri giggled and said, "Juice of the heart, always try to show respect."

When Annett left Norm and Aroonsri, she went looking for Bonnie and found her just as she and Andy were going into the Monark Mercantile.

Annett said to Bonnie, "I have seen the most luxuriant, the softest and best silk that I have ever laid my eyes on. That woman Aroonsri that will marry Norm, well, she has her wedding dress made out of this material, and it sure does look nice."

"Thank you for lookin after that; now everything is in order and ready."

"Bonnie said to Andy, "Sweetheart, can you excuse me for a moment; I want to go check on something."

"Sure will, I want to go look at this thorny wire."

Bonnie scampered over to the telegraph office to see if there was a message from Wild Bill.

Bernie said, "Good afternoon Bonnie, how are you?"

"I am top of the world, any messages for me from Wild Bill Hickok?"

"As a matter a fact, there is, here you are Bonnie." And he reaches over the desk and gives the message to Bonnie.

She hastily rips open the message envelope and reads, "Hello Bonnie; I hope everything is good STOP. I hate to say no, but I cannot come to Canada at this time STOP. I think next year I'll be ready to travel STOP. Will be good to see Hubert again STOP. Sorry I cannot come to your area at this time STOP. Your trusted friend Bill

Bonnie went over to the boarding house and checked to see if the Judge had arrived yet.

Sherry said, "Hi Bonnie, no, not yet, and I remember you're paying his boarding house bill."

"Thank you Sherry, and please don't tell Andy, this is a surprise for Andy, to see the Judge again."

Bonnie walked back to the mercantile thinking, "I sure hope the Judge can get in today."

Norm and Aroonsri sat down in Fred place for their supper. When the meal was brought to the table, Aroonsri took out a little bottle of what looked like red flakes, and she sprinkled this on her mashed potatoes.

Norm said, "What's that you're putting on your food?"

Aroonsri giggled and put a little bit of potato and meat on her spoon, lifted it up to Norm's mouth and said, "Here, eat this."

Norm took the potatoes and meat in his mouth; everything was OK for the first two or three bites, then all of a sudden, the more he chewed, the hotter it became. His mouth became so hot his face had become red, and all of a sudden Norm seemed to choke out the words, "WATER, WATER, I NEED WATER, OOHH THIS IS HOT." When Norm started to drink the water, he drank and drank and it felt like he couldn't get enough water.

Aroonsri laughed and laughed at Norm's red face and the amount of water he drank trying to cool his mouth down. Aroonsri said, "I'm sorry. I didn't mean to laugh so hard, but you did look a little funny, red face and all."

"That's OK, I should have known better, but WOW! That Was Hot!"

After supper Norm had suggested to Aroonsri, that they walk around Monark, Aroonsri took in all the sights and sounds of the town. Aroonsri thought she could like this town, and Norm was a person she could warm up to very easy, his easy going manner, yet he was strong in character and was always ready with a little laugh. She thought she could be the best wife for Norm; she would even do things for Norm the way she was taught back in her home in Siam, she would look after her man!

When they arrived back at Norm's house, Norm showed her to her room, said good night and went to his room, put water in the wash dish, had a wash then put on his nightshirt and crawled into bed. Norm drifted off to sleep easily and quickly.

At five o'clock in the evening, Fred got up, went to the livery, there he met Larry, and they saddled their horses and rode out to the Moonly Ranch. When they arrived at the Moonly Ranch, they put the horses in the corral, stripped the saddles and saddle bags from the horses, Fred took his saddlebags with all his cookin-spices he used for cookin, and took them to the cooking pit area.

Larry said, "Lookit this cooking spit, this is one fine looking contraption, whoever made this has done up a right fine job."

"Right you are young fellow if you unwrap the cow and slide the cow on this cookin-spit; I'll get ready to light the fire. I see they even have coal here to cook with as well as oak wood; this is a mighty fine lookin pit and spit area for cookin, they even put Andy's finest liquor by the pit for basting, a coffee pot with water and coffee here for us. "When the fire was burning, Fred said, "I'll need a pail of water from the well to mix my spices. When I start to lather the spices on the cow, we start turning this cow on the cookin-spit, we can't stop turning for too long."

Larry unwrapped the cow, Fred lit the fire, Larry fetched a pail of water and Fred put his cookin-spices in the pail of water and under the skin of the cow, then Larry started to turn the spit, the two started to cook the cow on the cookin-spit.

Bonnie woke at 5:00 o'clock in the morning the sun was just starting to show itself, she washed, dressed and rushed out to see Fred and Larry. As she walked up to Fred and Larry, she saw Larry turning the cookin-spit, and Fred was basting the cow. She said, "Good morning Fred, how is it coming?"

"The cow cookin is comin along very well, seasoning was placed under the skin and in the meat and basting with seasoning is working well, the cow will be very moist but cooked when we are done."

"I can smell the cooking product, and I must say if this tastes as good as it smells, then this will be one humdinger of a meal. Excuse me, Fred, I must go for breakfast and check on a few things."

I woke up at 5:30 in the morning; and started to fix breakfast, flapjacks with bee's honey. Aroonsri came out of her bedroom, and she was still in her sleeping clothes, she was rubbing her eyes as she came close to me. She walked up and gave me a hug and said "Good Morning."

"What would you like for breakfast?"

"May I have two eggs cooked hard not in the shell."

"I'm on it. We also have to leave here about 10:00 o'clock today to go out to the Moonly Ranch.

Bring your trunk with the clothes you want to be married in; you can change into your wedding clothes at the Moonly Ranch when the time comes. I'm sure Bonnie will let you use a bedroom in the house to change in."

"As soon as I eat, I'll change into my other clothes to wear out to where we are going; I'll wear a medium blue long shirt with black and pink flowers for design with black pants and silky white socks."

"HOOEEE! You will be the talk of the town, out at Moonly Ranch today many women will be so jealous because their husbands will be watching you. I'll wear my clean sheriff work duds, and I'll bring my Sunday go to church duds with me for our wedding out at Moonly's Ranch. I'm thinkin some of your sisters are going to be comin here to Monark, comin through that mail order bride service in that catalog that was started down East."

As soon as breakfast was over, Aroonsri and I washed and dried dishes then put them away; then we went to our separate bedrooms to get dressed.

18

A t The hotel, Judge Roy Bean woke up at 6 o'clock; he woke up his wife. They got dressed and went to Fred's place for Breakfast. After breakfast, they went to the livery stable for their horse and buggy and asked Bob Little to hitch the horse to the buggy, when that was done the Bean's started out for the Moonly Ranch. The Judge remembered the way to go from the last time he was here visiting Andy, many years ago. Roy thought to himself things haven't changed that much, more people maybe but that's all.

At the Moonly Ranch, everybody was in the dining room having breakfast, even Andy and Mark's mom and dad came out from Monark and stayed at the Moonly Ranch last night.

Andy said, "Dad, how is your bank, everything alright?"

"Since I bought that new safe to put in the bank, I have a secure bank. Now I have a safe that is almost impossible to break open. Now, I have no worries, and I sleep like a baby at night. Mom tells me now I'm so relaxed, I sound like a bull makin a noise ready to charge, I'm snoring so loud."

Bonnie said, "Andy, looks like everything is comin up good, all is ready for today, and oh, by the way, today your surprise package will come to the ranch!" then Bonnie giggle, and everybody but Andy, smiled and gave a little chuckle.

Andy said, "you gonna tell me, everybody but me knows about this?"

Mark chuckled and said, "Big brother, could be."

Just as they were finishing up breakfast, Bonnie said to the staff, "You have most of today off, we'll only ask for help if we get behind, OK."

All the staff agreed and said, "Thank you, ma'am."

Bonnie, Janet, Mark, and Andy washed, dried and put away the dishes.

Just as Andy was going out the door to check on Fred and Larry, the Parson rode up on his horse.

Andy said, "Good Morning Parson, William, can you put the Parson's horse in the corral. Parson would you like to come in and have a coffee."

"Thank you; I would like coffee, I feel a little parched this morning."

"Bonnie! Janet! The Parson is here. Excuse me, Parson, I have to go check on Fred."

Andy walked over to the cow cookin pit area to stand beside Fred. Larry and George came to help, they were moving slow, but cookin was still in progress.

Andy Said, "Good Morning Fred old buddy, Larry, and George how are you?. Fred, my old friend, how are you and your wife Chris doing?"

"Chris will be comin out to the ranch later, and she is doing fine. Cookin will be done in about 4 hours, feeling a little tired from cookin all night."

"You two are lookin a little rough around the edges." Andy pulled his watch out of his pocket and said "let's see, 7:30 in the morning, cookin will be done about 12:00 noon, just in time for lunch. Is there anything I can get for the three of you?"

"We have everything we need."

"At 10:00 o'clock, shootin competition starts, and Bonnie will look after the flour sack race at that time also; I have a horse up for first prize, for the best shot and Bonnie has a prize of new material to make a new dress for the flour sack race."

"You think Larry, George and I can get in on this shootin contest?"

"We'll make arrangements, as soon as you show up we'll get you shootin so that you can get back to a twistin the cookin-spit again."

Andy walked over to the shootin area and checked to see everything was set up there. He saw boxes of small clay plates that would be thrown in the air and many boxes of shotgun shells for the gun he had. All looked good here, Andy thought.

Mark came up to Andy and said, "What's it look like, everything in good order?"

"Little brother everything is comin together. Now I have to go and check with Bonnie and the Parson," and off Andy trod.

When Andy came up to Bonnie, she said, "Andy, you have to stay away from the shootin area until 10:30

this morning, until I have everything set up for you, promise me."

"Yes Bonnie, I will stay away, I'll go help Fred and the boys at cookin the cow."

"Andy, my dearest, thank you, sweetie."

"I also wanted to tell you, the cow will be done about 12 noon and looks like everything is ready for the clay plate shoot this morning, and the flour sack race for you ladies is all set. This contest should see who the best shot is. How about the Parson, is he already for both weddings, Ken will marry Lily and Norm will marry Aroonsri."

"Yes, Ken and Lily will be up front with the Parson first at 2:00 o'clock, then Norm and Aroonsri at 2:30in the afternoon. Everything is all set, the Parson is calm as lake water, and mind you Ken is shakin like a leaf in a spring gale."

"Glad to hear everything is comin together, Bonnie," and Andy walked off to the spit cookin area.

Bonnie found Mark and said "OK; everything is all coming together, Andy will stay in the cooking area until 10:30 this morning. The package should arrive here about 10:00 o'clock, can we hide Andy's surprise package in the house until Andy comes to the shooting area, then so Andy can't see the Judge, we can bring him up behind Andy to surprise him."

"I'm on it, oooeee, bro is going to be some surprised."

Just then Norm and Aroonsri drove up in their horse and buggy.

Bonnie said, "Aroonsri and Norm bring your clothes into the house, we'll hang them up, so they don't wrinkle, then Norm can you put your horse in the corral."

Norm and Aroonsri were walking hand in hand carrying their clothes, the Parson came out and said: "Norm, I have not seen that big of a smile on anyone in a long time."

"Parson, I heard someone use the words like a soul mate and life mate, I never believed in this until I met Aroonsri, now I found someone that I not only feel comfortable around, she also makes me feel like I am the only man in the world that matters to her. I have been missing her in my life all these years. The exact moment I had seen her, I fell in love with her. I fell, heart, mind, and soul, deeply in love with her. When I am around her, I feel like a teenage kid."

Then the Parson said, "Man and woman were not intended to be alone. We are all set to join two people today, two people that belong together, Congratulations; I'll see you two in front of me at 2:30 in the afternoon."

Just then, Mark saw the Slinger Ranch outfit come riding into the yard. Mark heard Hubert tell his ranch hands to tie the horses up on the right side of the corral.

Mark said, "Good morning, Hubert, I hope all is going well for you this morning."

"This day is going to be a great day, I can feel it."

Esther said to Hubert, "I am going to go look for my sisters and the Moonly girls."

"OK, see you a little later, I'll come to where you are when the lunch time comes, and also I'll find you when the weddings start."

As Esther was walking away, the McKlay Ranch outfit was comin into the yard.

Hubert said, "My outfit is tied up on the right side, outside of the corral area, why don't you take the left side."

Jim McKlay said, "Good idea, OK boys you heard it, tie your cayuse up on the left, outside of the corral."

Mark said, "Ken and Lily, both you carry your wedding clothes into the house, the girls will hang your clothes up, so they won't become wrinkled."

"OK, we're on it," Ken said.

"Where's Andy," Bob McKlay said, "I don't see him here."

Mark said, "Bonnie has him helping Fred cook the cow, so Andy won't see when the surprise package arrives for Andy."

"OOOEEE! He is going to be some surprised when all this takes place."

"Matter a fact I see Bonnie comin this way and look yonder, is that the Judge and his wife comin down the road?"

"By jigger, you have the eyes of a hawk, yes by cracky, you're right."

Mark said to Jack Tainan, "I see a horse and buggy comin down the road, I think this is Judge Roy Bean, a surprise for Andy, can you unhitch the horse from the buggy and put the horse in the corral when they stop."

"Yes boss, I'll go over to the corral right now and wait for them to stop and then give them directions."

When the horse and buggy stopped, Jack and William said: "Judge, sir, I'll look after your horse and buggy, Bonnie is waitin for you over there with Mark Moonly, and I don't see Hubert Slinger, I think he is walking around somewhere."

Jack and William unhitched the horse from the buggy, and they put the horse in the corral.

After Jack and William had put the horse in the corral, they came over to where Mark was standing.

Mark said, "OK Boys, it's almost time to start this shootin contest. William, can you go over to where the hole is dug, and get ready to throw those clay plates. Remember to throw only one at a time, throw only when someone yells THROW, and for pete's sake –don't forget, keep down low."

"Yes boss, I'm on it," said William.

Mark walked over to Fred and the boys cookin the cow; Mark said: "OK Fred, you and the boys come over to the shootin area, Andy can keep turnin on the spit while you're shooting in the competition."

Mark, Fred and the boys all walked over to the shootin area.

Mark said very loudly "OK FRED, YOU, LARRY AND GEORGE START THIS SHOOTIN OFF, FRED IS UP FIRST. William and Jack, are you ready?"

"Yes, We're Ready boss."

"OK Fred, when you are ready to fire, you need to yell, THROW, loudly and William will throw the clay plate one at a time, you have to shoot and hit 10 out of 10 plates to be a winner. In the end, if there is a tie, then we have more shooting, 40 out of 40 plates, understand? We have William in the pit; he is throwin the plates and Jack Tainan is taken the names down as well, writin the names and the score down."

"Got it, I'm ready. - - - THROW."

Meanwhile, at the house, Janet was coordinating Lily

and Aroonsri getting dressed and also putting their hair up in the hair design the ladies wanted.

Janet said "Don't worry, at lunch time we'll have food brought to us. Annett, Joan, and Esther will bring the food to us here in the house so we can eat in the dining room, the boys Norm and Ken will eat in the parlor, the boys are not to see the girls until the wedding starts."

Back at the shootin area, Fred, Larry, and George had finished shootin and were walking back to the cookin area, Fred had just shot 10 out of 10 clay plates.

When Andy had walked up to the shooting area, the time was now approximately 10:45 in the morning.

19

M ark grinned at Andy and said, "OK big brother, your turn, show them how to do it."

Andy picked up the shotgun, loaded the gun and yelled; "THROW!"

The clay dish went up and away from Andy, Andy threw the shotgun up to his shoulder, held it tight, led the clay dish a little bit. Andy gently squeezed the trigger; there was a loud roar, the shotgun sound exploded. The gun jerked backward with a violent thump into his shoulder, the end of the shotgun barrel bucked upward as the shotgun discharged. Only a small piece of the clay dish flew off the plate.

Behind Andy, somebody said, "I've seen little girl's shoot better than you do."

Andy heard that voice before, but where? Andy yelled, "THROW." then he slammed the shotgun to his shoulder, led the clay plate a little bit, Andy held his breath, he caressingly squeezed the trigger. The shotgun blasted a loud report, again the shotgun bucked and slammed backward into his shoulder, this time, half the clay plate disappeared. Behind him, he heard "I've seen my grandmother shoot better than you, at a longer distance."

Andy knew that voice, but where? Where had he heard that before? Andy said loudly "Who in tarnation is saying that this is a fun time for everyone!"

Andy turned around, looked, then his eyes grew big, his eyes seemed to grow big as coffee cups. Then Andy grasped one of the man's hands in both of his, pumped both of his hands vigorously up and down and said, "You old horse trader, how have you been? Judge, you are a sight that makes my eyes water! I haven't seen you in about eight years. HEY, EVERYBODY, I want you to meet my good and trusted friend Judge Roy Bean."

The Judge said, "Andy you old snake tamer, you are a sight for sore eyes, I do miss your smile, my friend, it is always good to see you and a bigger pleasure to be around you, I would surely like to pull a cork with you."

"Here Judge, I have three shots left, would you like to try your hand at this?"

"No thanks, I will take my turn later. I'm not lookin for any unfair advantage."

Mark said, "Andy, I have never known you to miss, what are you doin, are you feelin all right?"

"I'm leavin room for other people to take home a prize."

Hubert Slinger came up, and he shot 10 out of 10 plates, Hubert had shot without very much time in between shots, he proved again that he is a contender for the best shot prize.

The McKlay Brothers, Jim, and Bob came up; Bob had

nine out of ten plates shot and Jim had ten out of ten plates shot, all ten plates were a mist of dust when shot.

The cowhands came up and shot, and not one of them were able to get more than eight out of ten clay plates shot.

The Judge Roy Bean came up, each time he yelled THROW, when he shot, the shotgun was at hip level, and each time he shot the plate completely disappeared in a cloud of dust, with not even one small piece splintering off.

The Judge had a total of ten out of ten clay plates shot.

Mark said loudly for all to hear "OK NOW WE ARE DOWN TO A SHOOT OFF BETWEEN FRED BENSON, HUBERT SLINGER, JIM McKlay AND JUDGE ROY BEAN."

One of the bystanders went to fetch Fred to shoot.

Hubert shot, and he shot 39 out of 40 plates.

Jim Shot 40 out of 40 clay plates

Fred Benson shot 39 out of 40 clay plates.

Judge Roy Bean shot 40 out of 40 plates.

Mark Moonly took the center and said, "OK FOLKS, NOW WE HAVE A SHOOTOUT BETWEEN JIM McKlay AND JUDGE ROY BEAN, FIRST UP IS JIM WITH 60 SHOTS THEN THE JUDGE."

Jim checked his 60 shells; then he picked up the shotgun loaded the gun and yelled; "THROW!"

Each clay plate sailed through the air, up and to the rear. Jim brought the shotgun up and fired arithmetically at each plate as he yelled throw. Each time he shot, there was a loud explosion sound from the shotgun, a bluish color smoke, the gun bucked and slammed backward into Jim's shoulder. In all total, Jim shot 59 out of 60 plates; all 59 plates were a cloud of dust when hit.

The Judge came up, and he also fired the shotgun same as Jim did. Each time he yelled throw, he watched the clay plate sail up and away from him, and he led the plate just a mite. He would smash the shotgun up to his shoulder and hold tight; He would hold his breath, then caress the gun's trigger. Each time he fired, the clay plate disappeared into a burst of powder. The Judge had a total score of 60 out of 60 plates.

Mark took the center spot again and said loudly; "Judge Roy Bean has won the best shot competition."

Andy came up and said, "Judge, you have won the prize for the best shot. If you look yonder to the left, you will see a young 3-year-old horse tied up to a stake, that is the prize for the best shot."

The Judge came up and said "Andy, my old and good friend, I have never had such a good time as this, you have again made me feel welcome. I have never seen this before, shootin small plates for a prize, this is something new and exciting, and my esteem friend, you always seem to be able to make me smile in pure gratitude every time I see you thank you very much."

Bonnie came up to the group and said loudly, "In case you missed it, let me tell you how the women's flour sack race went. First, let me tell you that the flour sack race is fastened after the homesteaders, who use to have to walk to the country store, pick up the flour sacks and then walk back home.

Well, let me tell you, when the gun blasted, all the women started off on the run. They ran 50 feet to the left; there they picked up the flour sack. They had to run from there to the well and back to the house with the flour sack.

I had never seen anything look so easy, as when Annett took off on the run. Every time she took a running step she had lengthened the distance between herself and the other ladies. Annett grabbed that 50-pound flour sack, she tucked it under one arm, and then Annett took off like there was a fire comin at her. She passed the other women and came in first at the well, from there she was runin faster and leavin the other women farther behind. Annett McKlay has won the flour sack race. Annett McKlay wins the material for a new dress."

Then Andy said, "OOOEEE this is turnin out to be the best shindig ever. Everybody listen up, the food is ready, please go to the right side, outside of the house, you will find plates, knife, and fork as well as coffee, a bench, and tables to sit at and eat. After the meal, at 2 o'clock the weddings start with Ken and Lilly, and then follow up with Norm and Aroonsri."

First in line for the food was Annett, Esther, Joan and Janet with plates to fill for the girls getting ready. Next in line were 4 of the Moonly ranch hands to bring food to the men in the parlor.

Just as the rest of the guests started to fill their plates with meat and the potato cooked on the side of the fire, and the carrots and parsnips from the cooking pots, Daryl McFidgen rode into the Moonly Ranch. He was wearing his Police Uniform with the big Stetson hat, when he rode into the yard, he was an exhibition all in itself. After he had put his horse in the corral, he walked up to Jim and Bob McKlay and said, "I wouldn't miss this for anything. I've known Norm and Ken for many years; I feel this is important not only for me but more important, them two men who are my friends, I had to attend."

Jim said, "Welcome and glad you could make it, better go over and fill your plate up with meat, potatoes, vegetables, and fresh buns are on the table."

"OK, thanks, I'll head that way now."

Hubert saw Daryl ride into the Moonly Ranch; he walked over to Daryl and said, "Glad you could make it down here. I have a horse picked out for you to take back to Calgras with you. This horse is my design of horse flesh. If the Police force like the horse flesh, then you can pay me and buy more. I have also found out what happened to all your other horses, why they died, why they went loco and had to be shot, they had what is called swamp fever. Swamp fever is caused by drinking different water and even goes so far as eating different grass. You have to give only little bits of water and grass to the horse when traveling to different areas that are great distances away. This new strain of horse flesh will be much hardier than you are used to, and yet they are a purebred. Let me know how the Police officers like this horse flesh. Now you better go eat."

Meanwhile, the ladies in the house were all getting ready, and they were all just about finished. The two ladies getting married, never, had they went through such rigorous help to make them look absolutely exquisite. Lily and Aroonsri were both breath taken beautiful when they were gazed upon. The ladies had fixed Lily's and Aroosri's hair so that the hair would complement the wedding dress.

The Parson said, "Daryl McFidgin, please go get Ken McKlay and bring him here."

"I'm on it."

Then the Parson said, "Bonnie you go get Lily Malone, wait until Ken is standing here, then bring her here, and remember to walk slowly."

"I'm on my way to do that now, and yes, I will remember."

Ken stood up first with the parson; he was shaking like a leaf in the wind. Ken stood there with the parson and Daryl, all three looking towards the house. When Lily first showed up, her white wedding dress looked so nice and seemed to be shimmering in the sunlight, her face was so beautiful to look at, and there were tears coming down Ken's face.

Ken whispered to Daryl, "Look at her, I never knew she was so beautiful, I knew she was beautiful, but look at her, WOW!"

The parson took both their hands in his and said; "These two people have come together for marriage, does anybody disagree, if no one disagrees let no one tear asunder. The Parson then tied Lily's and Ken's left hand together with is parson's scarf. Lily Malone, do you take Ken McKlay to be your lawful wedded husband, to honor and obey, in sickness and in health for the rest of your life for as long as you live?"

"I do."

"Ken McKlay, do you take Lily Malone as your wedded wife in sickness and health for the rest of your life for as long as you live?"

"I-I-I d-d-do." Ken stammered

"By the power invested in me, and in front of God,

I pronounce you Husband and Wife. I introduce Mister Ken McKlay and Misses Lily McKlay."

Well, there was a clappin goin on like you never hear before and everybody laughing and cheering, they were clapping Ken on his back and congratulating Lily!

The Parson said, "OK, settle down, Daryl, would you go get the Sheriff Norman John and bring him here to stand in front."

"I'm on it,"

"Bonnie, would you go get Aroonsri and bring her here to stand in front."

Norm and Daryl walked out of the house and came up to stand in front by the parson.

First, Bonnie came out of the house and about 10 feet away from the house, Bonnie waited for Aroonsri. Aroonsri finally came out of the house and slowly walked up to Bonnie.

Norm watched Aroonsri walk up to Bonnie, and as she got to Bonnie, Norm's mouth dropped open, there he stood slack jawed, then his legs gave away, and Daryl had to hold him up.

Daryl looked at Norm, and there were big droplet tears running down Norm's face.

Norm said, "Have you ever seen any woman look so beautiful; she is beyond exquisite!"

Norm watched Aroonsri come gliding toward him; he saw her wearing her hair up high with only a few strands hanging loose, her face was just a shade of white, with her lips well formed and colored red. He saw the finest, richest, most ornate pink silk dress with white elephants with the elephant truck pointing at an angle upward all over her dress, and the shining black shoes that looked so small, and yet she looked like she was floating across the grass toward him. Her eyes were shining like he had never seen shine before, just like somebody holding a candle to see the sparkle of a thousand diamonds, shining in a mirror and he looked at her eyes shining, and there he stood with his mouth open.

When Aroonsri finally reached Norm he was sure he had a thousand butterflies in his stomach, he was shaking all over with excitement of seeing how beautiful she looked, Norm had never in his life or wildest dreams, had he ever seen anybody look so beautiful.

The parson was asking a question of Norm, but his voice seemed so far away, and he couldn't concentrate, he could only look at Aroonsri in wonder. Then the Parson touched Norm's hand, and he came out of his mesmerized shock.

The Parson said, "Please give me your hands."

Norm and Aroonsri raised their left hands up to the parson.

"Is there anyone who says these two should not become joined together in marriage?"

No one answered.

The parson took his scarf from around his neck and wrapped to scarf around Aroonsri's and Norm's hand, and it looked like he had tied their hands together, and then he said "This represents the bond between Norm and Aroonsri from this day forward, let no one tear it apart.

Arounsri Gornphun, do you take Norman John to be your lawful married husband in sickness and health, to love, honor and obey for the rest of your life for as long as you shall live?"

"I do."

Norman John, do you take Aroonsri Gornphun for your lawfully wedded wife in sickness and health, to love, honor and cherish for the rest of your life for as long as you shall live?"

"I do."

"By the power invested in me, I now pronounce you husband and wife. I introduce Mister Norman John and Misses Aroonsri John!"

Judge Roy Bean rushed up, clapped Norm on the back, shook his hand and said to Aroonsri: "Young lady, you have done something nobody else could do, you have hog tied Norman, I congratulate you and Norm, well done. If Norm ever gives you a hard time, or Norm ever makes you cry, you send me a telegram, and I'll drop what I'm doin, and I'll come a runnin to help you!"

There were many people coming up to congratulate Norman and Aroonsri.

Andy Moonly said very loudly "HELP THE PIE-ANIE PLAYER SETUP THE PIE-ANIE, MAKE ROOM FOR LANCE JOHN WITH HIS SQUEEZE BOX AND BILL MOONLY WITH HIS FIDDLE AND THE MAYOR - DAVE MILNER TO CALL THE DANCE. I DECLARE THIS DANCE TO BE STARTED. EVERYONE IS REQUIRED TO HAVE A GOOD TIME. THE TWO WEDDING COUPLES HAVE TO START THE DANCE.

Andy reflected about today, he thought about the packages that have arrived. The package from Siam sure did look good standing up front with Norman John. What a gift, the Judge came to see me and more. Now it's my turn to get Bonnie and have a good time; tomorrow will be another day. You never know, someday we may go to see the Judge. I'm startin to feel the itch to see other places.

The author, Norman John Rumpel was born in a little town in Saskatchewan, Canada, Sept 15, 1950. At the age of 10 to 14, he would go out to his uncle's farm and pick stones, help with bailing, help with the farm chores and harvest in the summer. Norm did everything from feed pigs, milk cows by hand, herd cows on foot, drive a tractor pulling a binder in the fall, stooking sheaves after bindering was completed. At the age of 19, Norm left home, joined the military and spent 21 years in the Canadian Armed Forces. While in the military Norm owned horses, and at that time, he even rode an unbroken horse, he broke that horse to ride for a little girl. In the military Norm had traveled from the west coast of Canada to the east coast of Canada and North near the North Pole and South to the 49th parallel. After the military, he had many jobs ranging from driving a tractor trailer, building pig barns to working in Afghanistan supporting the Canadian and United States of America Military. If you ever ask Norm where was the best place? He will answer, "When I retired, I stayed at home, and stayed very close to and beside my best friend who is also my wife."

Printed in the United States
By Bookmasters